THE HERMIT OF HART'S HOLLOW

•

Gail MacMillan

AVALON BOOKS
NEW Y

D1364991

PRINTED IN THE UNITED STATES OF AMERICA
ON ACID-FREE PAPER
BY HADDON CRAFTSMEN, BLOOMSBURG, PENNSYLVANIA

To Steve and his own special Michelle, on their
engagement.

Chapter One

"Hold the light higher, Mitch! We haven't got much time!"

The two figures swathed from head to toe in cat-burglar black leaned over the drawer of the file cabinet and strained to see the labels on the manila folders inside. The shorter one stretched on tiptoes in response to the order, slender form trembling.

"Ken, this isn't right! Let's just go!" she pleaded in a whisper.

"Be quiet and hold the light steady!" her companion hissed. "We'll be out of here in a couple of minutes with all the evidence we need to nail this guy and break a front-page story!"

A shrill whistle suddenly rent the air.

"What's that?" She gasped, her heart seeming to rocket to the back of her throat and lodge there.

"Security!" The man slammed the drawer shut, barely missing her black-gloved fingers. "Run!"

He whirled and headed for the door they had left slightly ajar for their escape. She tried to follow but her foot caught in a computer cord and she was sent sprawling onto the thick rug. Her ankle twisted as she went down and she cried out in pain.

"Ken, help me!" She gasped, struggling to get to her feet. "Ken . . ."

But her companion had fled.

"Hey, what's going on in there?" A security guard appeared, a looming dark outline in the doorway. A moment later he was dragging her to her feet. Police officers arrived shortly and all the inherent indignities of arrest followed. . . .

Three days later Mitch Wallace still cringed when she thought of the night of February sixth in that Toronto office complex. With a deep sense of gratitude, however, she also remembered Captain Jarvis Matheson, the officer in charge at the police precinct. He had recognized her as a reporter, knew her father, and had been quick to help her find a way out.

"That Councilor Giverson is a slime ball," he'd said as Mitch, feeling giddy and nauseated, had sat before him in his spanking-new office. "I wish you had been able to get evidence that would put him away. The vice boys have been trying to get at him for months. Our problem now, however, is how to get you out of this mess as quietly and painlessly as possible. I assume you don't want Joe and your mother to know."

"Dad? Never!" The thought horrified Mitch almost as much as her arrest. "He'd be devastated! His business would be ruined!"

"I've thought of that." Capt. Matheson had leaned a hip into his polished oak desk. "Joe's construction company does a lot of work for the city, doesn't it? His guys did a bang-up job renovating this old place last fall. If news of what you tried to do to a councilor gets out, it could jeopardize any chance he might have at future municipal contracts.

"I think I can get the security guard to keep quiet . . . he's a former cop." Matheson had run a hand through his thinning hair. "But there could be leaks elsewhere. It would be best if you just dropped out of sight for a while. Is that possible? Can you think of an excuse to leave town? Somewhere to go?"

Profoundly grateful, Mitch could only nod. Then she had followed his suggestions to the letter. She had placed a hastily written letter of resignation dated, as Capt. Matheson suggested, at 5:15 P.M. that afternoon, on her editor's desk, sent an e-mail message to her parents in the suburbs, packed at her city apartment, and by dawn had been on her way to the family cottage in northern New Brunswick with her dog Sadie as her companion.

The reason she had given for her sudden departure had been simple: she had to have solitude to write a book she'd been contemplating for months and could no longer contain. She hadn't had to repeat the lie to Ken Clark. He had not tried to contact her. Mitch was confident he had decided that distancing himself from her would keep him in the clear.

Just as she was about to leave the precinct, however, Capt. Matheson had surprised her with some advice regarding her former colleague.

"I'd steer clear of your old partner, Kenny Clark, if I were you," he'd said. "He's trouble.

I haven't got all the details yet but I've learned he was responsible for this mess you're in."

Mitch had averted her eyes, reluctant even in the face of what Ken had done to her to incriminate him. After all, she had thought they were in love.

"I don't expect you to finger him." Capt. Matheson had seemed to read her mind. "I know you were more than colleagues. And, mind you, I'm not saying he isn't a real crusader—probably will be responsible for putting more than a few crooks out of business before he moves into an editor's chair. It's his methods I call to task. He gets so intent on the end results he doesn't stop to ponder if the means are justifiable."

"I hear you, Captain," Mitch had replied. "Consider your advice taken."

And she had. She'd left Toronto without attempting to get in contact with Ken and with the book-writing story as her reason. At the time the former had seemed the most difficult. Now, as she stared at the cursor blinking mockingly at her from the computer screen, she wondered if that was indeed the case. She hadn't a single idea for a story. Yet come spring, she would be expected back in Toronto with some kind of manuscript to validate her absence.

The truth definitely couldn't be allowed to surface. If it did, her father's business would be ruined. Joe Wallace, through years of hard work, had risen from a country carpenter to the head of his own huge construction company. He had worked sixteen-hour days, frequently ignoring weekends and holidays, to build his firm. These days his major client was the City of Toronto. Mitch knew the mayor and councilors would not be eager to offer future construction contracts to a man whose only child had been caught red-handed burglarizing the office of a colleague.

"What am I going to do, Sadie?" She looked down at the little red fox-like dog sitting on the floor beside her chair. "I haven't even a shadow of a plot in mind."

The dog, a Nova Scotia duck-tolling retriever, whined sympathetically and raised a white front paw to place it comfortingly on Mitch's knee.

"Thanks, babe." She smiled at her companion's unfailing faith. "You've always been my biggest supporter. Maybe we should take a break. This writer's block doesn't appear in danger of dissolving any time soon. Let's go down to the store and pick up a newspaper. I'll bet Geraldine has one of those special dog biscuits you like so much. When we get back, we'll send Mom and Dad our daily e-mail to let them know we're okay. Heaven knows they were upset enough by our sudden leaving. We have to be careful not to worry them further."

Sadie jumped to her feet, white-tipped tail whisking, and gave a quick, sharp bark.

"Okay, okay, let's go," she said, rubbing the little dog's ears. "You're as clever as you are cute. If you keep catching on at this rate, by next winter you'll be able to talk."

Mitch arose, stretched, and pushed golden-blond hair back from her face. Then she paused to look out at the winter hinterland beyond the window. When she had arrived at the cottage the previous afternoon, she had set up her computer in the corner window of the kitchen that afforded a view of the country road that ended in her dooryard, some of the lofty pines that sheltered the little building, and, through them, a glimpse of the frozen river beyond.

The scene would have been postcard perfect if it hadn't been marred by a single flaw. Someone had recently driven a snowmobile over the river's frozen surface. The machine had left a tractor trail that looked like a giant zipper for as far as Mitch could see along the snow-covered ice.

She frowned. Those tracks annoyed her, evidence that someone was invading her space.

Then she shook her head ruefully and reached for her gloves. Who exactly did she think she was to feel intruded upon? She didn't own the entire country. That snowmobiler had as much right to be there as she did. Her love of this beautiful, unspoiled place was making her selfish. Coming back to where she had spent so many happy days as a child had simply awakened such warm and wonderful memories she didn't want anyone or anything to infringe upon them. Not now. Not when she desperately needed the reassurance of cherished times to kill the bitter pain of betrayal still strong in her mind.

Her bogus reason for returning to New Brunswick hadn't gone down easily with local shopkeeper Geraldine Morrison, however, Mitch recalled as she checked her purse to make sure she had her wallet. The elderly owner of the only store within a twenty-mile radius of Mitch's cottage had been skeptical about the young woman's reasons for deserting Toronto life for an isolated cottage at road's end in this small, out-of-the-way community in February.

"People don't come down here to hibernate in midwinter for no reason, especially not pretty young women with careers well under way," the crusty seventy-plus-year-old woman had said bluntly when Mitch had first arrived and stopped her Tracker at the store for gas and groceries. "Unless they're running away from something . . . or someone."

She'd looked shrewdly over her glasses as she paused in adding up Mitch's bill in a receipt book.

"Come on, Geraldine." Mitch, who had known the inquisitive old lady all her life, had simply laughed. "I told you. I need peace and quiet to write my novel. Nothing more."

Her heart had fluttered a bit, however, at the woman's remarks. Geraldine was possessed of an uncanny perceptiveness, always had been. She would have to be very careful around the shrewd old lady, Mitch realized as she looked about the kitchen for her sunglasses. The comfortable old room was papered with a pattern of faded wildflowers and had chipped white cupboards around two of its walls. In its center was a rock maple dining set whose once-glowing finish was only a memory. Along the third wall, a round-cornered refrigerator sat beside a spanking-new electric range that only last summer had replaced a vintage gas one.

The cottage had been her parents' first home after they had married twenty-seven years ago, Mitch recalled as she found her Ray-Bans on the window ledge near the back door. Joe Wallace had built it for the bride he hoped to win, the daughter of one of the wealthy families who owned a summer place in the village. And win her he had, in spite of her parents' protests. He and Elise had married and lived for a few years in the cottage until a lucrative job opportunity had presented itself in Ontario. Then they had moved away, a tiny daughter by that time a member of their family. Although Joe Wallace had become a wealthy Toronto contractor by his mid-forties, he and his wife preferred to keep their New Brunswick hideaway humble and cozy. Each summer they returned and Mitch had always felt her parents, in spite of the luxurious lifestyle they had achieved in Toronto, were happiest there.

Maybe, she thought as she wandered through the archway from the kitchen to the living room, that was partially why she had chosen to come there in her exile—to try to recapture a bit of the peace and contentment she and her parents had always found living in the cottage.

As Mitch entered the room, sunlight was streaming in through the wide, multipaned picture window to warm the scratched oak floor beneath her gray-socked feet. Its years of handiwork was apparent in the faded couch and easy chairs that, in the early seventies, had sported a gaudy gold-and-brown floral design. Wear and strong, natural lighting, however, had muted and mellowed their vibrant hues to a shabby softness that gave Mitch a sense of comfort and security.

A mahogany coffee table, a copy of *How to Recognize an Inspiration* on one corner and whose edges had been a resting place for nearly thirty years for feet both bare and booted, also shared in the late afternoon rays. In the front corner near the window a tall, narrow book overflowed with a mother's and daughter's eclectic collection of literature. Both Mitch and her mother were voracious readers, devouring everything from contests on cereal boxes to Shakespeare.

Mitch smiled as she thought about her mother: beautiful, blond, blue-eyed Elise whose high spirits and loving compassion never wavered and never ceased to delight the big, gentle man she had married. She'd turned her back on a life of wealth and physical ease to marry the quiet, amiable country carpenter and move into this small, rustic cottage. Mitch had never once heard her express any regrets. A photo between two hurricane lamps on the mantelpiece of the big fieldstone fireplace that dominated the right wall showed Elise Wallace seated on the cottage steps, smiling tenderly as she cradled baby Michelle lovingly in her arms.

Mitch's father had told her that he and her mother had used those same oil lamps and fireplace for light and heat during their first winter together when they had lived in the cottage without benefit of electricity. His gray eyes had lost their usual alert intensity, softening into gentle crinkles at the corners from remembered happiness as he spoke.

Reaching for her boots and jacket, Mitch felt nostalgically wistful. To be in love like that in a place like this must have been pure magic. She picked up her keys and headed out to her Tracker. Too bad it was no longer possible. Ken Clark had taught her the unreality of long-term, trustworthy love in unforgettable terms.

Shoving his memory aside as best she could, Mitch gave herself over to the enjoyment of the ten-mile drive to the little country store. She passed through an area sparsely populated with hobby farms and seasonally deserted summer homes. Fields wore blankets of perfect white that shimmered in the sunlight. Evergreens flaunted ermine robes that glinted and sparkled in stark contrast to the bare arms of the birches and maples that formed delicate lacy patterns against the cloudless blue sky. Mitch smiled behind her tinted glasses as she looked over at Sadie, contentedly belted into the passenger seat.

"Lovely, isn't it, girl?" she said. "If a person can't get inspired here, they're hopeless."

When Mitch pulled in at the faded little country store a few minutes later, four trucks were stopped at the gas pumps, snowmobiles both in their cargo spaces and on their trailers. Geraldine, in an ancient one-piece ski suit, was bustling about, pumping fuel and keeping up a steady stream of talk with her customers. Mitch parked her vehicle out of the way of the transient group, released Sadie, and got out. The little dog bounded eagerly after her.

"I'll see you inside," Mitch responded to Geraldine's welcoming wave, and headed into the store.

Whoever decided sixty-five was retirement

age had never met Geraldine Morrison. Although the woman admitted to being over seventy, Mitch guessed she was also over seventy-five. No more than five foot two inches tall and rail thin, the little woman had a face as weathered as her store and was as tough as the proverbial nails.

As Mitch walked toward the door, she realized Geraldine and her store had a lot more in common than appearance. The building's faded rectangular facade concealed a sharp pitched roof perfectly suited to deal with the onslaught of winter snows and any other problems the years and elements might throw its way. Weather-worn and unpretentious, it had withstood the coming of supermarkets in the fifties and more recently superstores in the town a mere forty-minute drive away, and still maintained its integrity as a place that offered almost anything a person could need in necessary consumables.

"Folks around here depend on me to have what they need," Geraldine had once proudly told Mitch. "They trust me."

Trust. The word implied dependability and caring commitment. As strong as steel and as fragile as china, it definitely could not be applied to someone she had recently cared for.

But that was old news. She shrugged off the memory as she pulled open the store's sagging aluminum storm door, pushed aside the ancient wooden one that still stuck in the same way it had when she was a child, grinned as the bell on top tinkled familiarly, and stepped into the store's shabby interior.

Mitch was surprised to find it deserted, Usually it was a gathering place, an unofficial community center where local residents met to discuss everything from international politics to the latest in corn plasters. And they told stories. She remembered herself in shorts, T-shirt, braids, and bare feet hiking her ten-year-old self up onto the old counter and listening, enthralled, as jokes, gossip, yarns, and bits of local legends and wisdom flowed around her. It had been then she'd developed her love of stories, fact as well as fiction.

She felt a nostalgic smile curling her lips as she remembered Ben Robinson telling about his amazing border collie that had once—so he said—treed a cougar. And old Archie Manderson sitting on the edge of the dusty display window, smoking his pipe and telling the story of the ghost of the headless nun who wandered community back roads on dark and stormy nights. And there had been Sam Foley, who

would limp into the store each day accompa-
nied by Bob, his equally lame crow. He had
rescued Bob from a trap years before and the
bird had become his devoted companion.

Local ladies visited too; not lingering as
long as the men but long enough to exchange
news, gossip, and recipes as they shopped.
Elise had tried many of their cooking ideas
during her summers in the community and had
told Mitch some of them were better than
dishes she'd had when she had traveled with
her parents in Europe before her marriage.

Of course, Geraldine always presided, listening gravely, nodding or talking as the situation
warranted or offering a wise or droll solution.

At the moment, however, Mitch was glad to
be alone to savor the store's reassuring ambience. Geraldine's place always had a soothing
effect on her, reminding her that she was home
safe and sound. From the narrow strips of
warped hardwood that formed floor and ceiling
to the tin filigree wall borders and worn-to-
gentle-waves counter, it exuded an atmosphere
of age and stability.

The old general store also offered a wide
variety of home, farm, and fishing supplies. A
little bit of this, a little bit of that. Mitch
hummed a tune as she absently examined a

dusty display of fishing lures Geraldine had not gotten around to putting away for the winter and basked in the mingling odors of old wood and spices. Then, wandering toward the back of the store, she was delighted to catch the aroma of Geraldine's famous homemade cookies. Wafting out from behind a curtained doorway that led to the shop owner's living quarters was the unmistakable, mouthwatering scent of peanut butter dreams. Mitch drew a deep breath. Yes, she was home again.

As a child, whenever she had been feeling a little blue or out of sorts, her parents would bring her to Geraldine's for cookies. Sometimes, if Geraldine was actually baking when they arrived, Mitch would convince her parents to leave her there to help. Soon, between the batter and the chatter, Mitch would find her happiness returning. She shook her head sadly and wished a batch of cookies could solve her problems now.

Absently she strolled back to the counter where a huge roll of brown paper in a black, ornate cast-iron holder topped with a spool of twine explained the way Geraldine still packaged purchases. Several books of punch-out children's valentine cards were propped up against it.

Mitch glanced idly through the little greetings for a moment, then with a sigh set them aside. She definitely wasn't in the hearts-and-flowers mood this year.

Then she noticed a copy of the *National Mail* on the far corner of the counter. Recalling that she'd made the trip not only to escape her computer but also to get a paper, she picked it up. Halfway down the front page an article immediately caught her attention. Or, at least the byline KEN CLARK did.

So you finally made it onto the front page, did you? she thought sardonically. *Well, good for you. I wonder how many bodies besides mine you walked over to get there.*

Her gaze wandered half-interestedly over the story about a famous science fiction writer who had gone missing. His publisher was offering a sizable reward for information regarding his whereabouts. Mitch made a face. If she knew anything about Ken Clark, he was probably already hot on the trail.

"Now, Michelle, what can I do for you, honey?" Geraldine broke in on her thoughts as the elderly woman entered, stamping snow from her boots and unzipping her snowsuit.

"We just came down for a newspaper, a little conversation, and hopefully, one of those special dog biscuits." Mitch pulled herself out of her troubling reflections and grinned at her friend.

"Well, no problem, there." Geraldine removed her boots and stepped clear of her outerwear. Underneath she was dressed in a pair of brown polyester pants, a daisy print blouse, and a shabby gray cardigan she had worn on cold days for as long as Mitch could remember.

"Where is everyone today?" Mitch asked. "There's usually a lively discussion of some sort under way. I'm surprised to find the place empty."

The shopkeeper hung up her suit, pulled a beige toque from her curly gray hair, and retrieved her glasses from where they had been dangling on a chain about her neck.

"All gone home," she replied. "Radio's predicting a blizzard—the 'storm of the century,' some stations are forecasting. My regulars bought up everything they thought they could possibly need in an emergency and headed home to batten down the hatches. Like those snowmobilers I was just serving.

"Now," she said, placing her glasses on her nose, and proceeded behind the counter to squint underneath it. "Biscuits."

Sadie let out an eager bark and braced all four paws squarely on the floor in front of the counter, ready to catch the treat.

Mitch laughed. "By this time next year, I've predicted she'll be talking, Geraldine. I wish I were half as clever."

"Now what's that supposed to mean?" Geraldine found the dog biscuits and flipped one to Sadie. The little dog caught it expertly and went to lie down on an old hand-woven rug in a corner to enjoy it.

"I don't know what I'm going to do," Mitch confessed, leaning her hips back against the scarred old counter, arms and ankles crossed in front of her. "I just can't get started on my book." She shook her head sadly and looked over at Sadie munching contentedly.

"Well, if this is going to be a serious discussion, we'd better get ourselves fortified first." The storekeeper bustled through the curtained doorway and reappeared shortly with a tray holding two tall glasses of cold milk and a plate of peanut butter dreams.

"You always knew the secret to cheering me up, Geraldine." Mitch picked up a glass in one hand and a golden-brown cookie in the other. "Now if you can just come up with a story idea, everything will be perfect."

"Hmmm." Geraldine pursed the sunburst of wrinkles about her thin lips into a tight little pucker and furrowed her forehead. "Exactly what do you think might get you going? A major catastrophe, or a visit from aliens, or . . ."

"Nothing quite so dramatic." Mitch found herself chuckling in spite of her problem. "Just one good solid hero; a tall, handsome man with a mysterious past would do for a start."

"Hmmm." Geraldine placed her palms on the counter's bumpy surface and swayed back and forth for a few moment. Then she came to a halt, her weathered face brightening. "What about the hermit up at Hart's Hollow? I don't know if he's handsome under that beard and long hair, but he sure has a mysterious past. No one around here knows the first thing about him."

"Hermit?" Mitch's tone lit up with interest and she hoisted herself up to settle comfortably on the counter near the storekeeper to listen. "A genuine people-shunning, cabin-dwelling hermit? This could be just what I'm looking for. Tell me all you know about him."

"I don't know much." Geraldine, glad to have interested Mitch enough to keep the young woman's company a while longer in a store low on customers during the winter months, settled back on an old oak stool to talk. "He came here in the fall driving a rental truck—you know, one of those big, closed-in rigs you can put a whole house full of furniture inside. He was moving into the old Buchanan cabin up in Hart's Hollow, he said when he stopped here to gas up. And that's about all I could get out of him.

"From what I've heard from some of the fellas who've gone upriver since, he's settled in real good. He must have returned the truck. They say there's no sign of any vehicle around the place, so it seems he doesn't plan to come out for a spell. He must have had a heap of supplies and had really decided to become a sure-enough hermit."

"Tell me what he looked like." Mitch leaned eagerly toward the storekeeper. "Every little detail."

"Well . . ." Geraldine tapped a finger reflectively against her nose. "He was tall—at least six feet—and had a nice set of shoulders, and . . ."

"And?" Mitch pressed.

"And he looked real good in those jeans." Geraldine chuckled, winking at her young friend. "For his age."

"His age? How old is he?" Mitch felt the

edge go off her excitement. She had been hoping for a reasonably youthful hero, below forty years of age.

"Well . . ." Geraldine again tapped her nose. "That long gray hair and beard probably aged him, but his eyes . . ."

"What about his eyes?" Mitch's enthusiasm arose once more. "Were they fierce, angry, mocking, hurt . . . ?"

"No, no, none of those," the storekeeper replied. "More . . . tired, weary, maybe, but . . ."

"Jaded?" Mitch supplied eagerly. "World weary, woman weary?"

"Yes, yes, that's it!" Geraldine jumped to her feet. "Jaded!"

"Ah-ha!" Mitch slid off the counter and clapped her hands, making Sadie jump alert and ready to her feet. "A man of the world who finally meets the perfect woman . . . only she turns out to be engaged in industrial espionage . . . or maybe she's a movie star so self-absorbed there's no room for anyone else in her life. He's deeply wounded by her deception or disinterest or whatever, and comes here to get away from the world, determined never to love again! Geraldine, this is great! Tell me more. What profession do you think he was in?"

"Now how would I know?" Geraldine replied. "He wasn't exactly wearing a badge."

"Well, then, what did he look as if he did?" Mitch pressed, leaning over the counter toward the store owner. "Were his hands suntanned and callused or pale and smooth? Hands provide lots of clues."

"Suntanned with short, clean nails, professional manicure," Geraldine said quickly. "I noticed when he paid me for the gas . . . with cash."

"A wealthy man who has time to enjoy the sun." Mitch was piecing him together like a jigsaw puzzle. "And yet he gave it all up to come here, to hide from the world. Oh Geraldine, you've just given me the inspiration I need! Now all I have to do is meet this man of mystery! I'll just snowshoe up to Hart's Hollow and—."

"Now just a minute, young lady." Geraldine crossed her arms on her chest. "I don't think you should go racing after the man. He's a hermit. That means he doesn't want visitors, especially not ones trying to delve into his past. And what I said about his eyes—"

"Yes, yes." Mitch was impatient, buttoning her jacket to leave.

"Well . . ." Geraldine glanced apprehensively about into the late-afternoon shadows gathering in the corners of the old store and hugged her cardigan more tightly about her.

"Oh, for heaven's sake, Geraldine, stop looking so furtive and tell me! What about his eyes?"

"When I started asking him a few questions—only a few, mind you—his eyes turned hard and cold and downright suspicious. He was almost rude, telling me to mind my own business in not exactly those words."

"Intriguing." Mitch pulled on her gloves and turned toward the door. "I can't wait to meet him."

"Hold on, young lady." Geraldine rounded the counter with a speed amazing for her age and caught Mitch by the arm. "Don't you get any crazy ideas about going up to Hart's Hollow alone. Not with this storm on the way. And definitely not without knowing more about the man. For all we know, he could be a serial killer!"

Chapter Two

Mitch stepped out of her bathroom, and glanced toward the kitchen, and screamed. A massive black figure with a bulbous head stood silhouetted in the lamplight just inside her back door. Sadie, whose wild barking had summoned her from the shower, was dancing madly around the creature, snarling.

Terrified, Mitch tried to retreat back into the steamy room but the creature was too quick. Long, swift strides brought it almost instantly to her side. Its huge black paw shot out to seize her by one arm.

"Let me go!" she yelled. She tried to wrench free but its strength was far beyond hers.

"Take it easy!" a voice muffled behind a

Plexiglas visor ordered. "I'm not going to hurt you! I'm a camp patrol officer."

"Oh, right!" she cried back. "And I'm the Easter Bunny!"

But she did stop struggling, partly because she'd realized he was only a snowmobiler in full protective attire, but mostly because the belt of her robe had loosened in the struggle and ends of the towel she'd hastily wound about her wet hair were beginning to flap free into a pattern not unlike a pair of limp rabbit ears.

"You'd better have some state-of-the-art ID, buddy!" She finished trying to muster some dignity as she haughtily adjusted her clothing.

"I do, I do," he muttered, releasing her. He pulled off his helmet and fumbled in his jacket pocket. "Just get this little fox or whatever it is off my leg!"

Wavy black hair and sapphire-blue eyes suddenly trimmed one of the handsomest faces Mitch had ever seen. The only flaw she could find in its strong, clean-shaven features was the amused expression it wore looking down at her.

Oh, great! she thought. Another break-and-enter artist with drop-dead good looks. Just what I need!

"It's okay, Sadie," she said. "You can let him go. But if he makes any suspicious moves, kill! Who *are* you?" she continued, returning her attention to the stranger.

"Dan Jeffrey." He managed to pull a laminated ID from his pocket and handed it to her. "This cottage has been vacant since I started this job. When I saw lights tonight, I thought I'd better check it out. Sorry I scared you."

"What makes you think you scared me?" Mitch stepped back and adjusted the shawl collar of her white terry-cloth robe more snugly about her throat as she examined the bit of plastic. Signed by Constable Bradley Stuart, who she knew was a member of the local detachment of the Royal Canadian Mounted Police, it confirmed that Dan Jeffrey was an authorized camp patrol officer.

"Well, I'm assuming that you don't normally step out of your bathroom and scream." Blue eyes glinting with amusement twinkled down on her and she felt the corners of her lips curling into a little shamefaced smile.

"Since I don't recall your ever having been around on such previous occasions, you can't really be certain, can you?" She couldn't resist a comeback.

"Touché." He grinned and bent to pat a now-

inquisitive Sadie. The dog sniffed him carefully, then slowly began to wag her tail.

"Do you live near here?" she asked, deciding
he must be all right if Sadie liked him. "You
must pass this cottage often to know that it's
been vacant for a while."

"I check it regularly along with all the oth-
ers," he said, straightening up to all of his six-
foot height and looking down at her. "It's my
job. I travel from cottage to cottage and camp
to camp to make sure no break-ins or any other
irregularities have occurred while they're not
occupied."

"Then I guess I should thank you." Mitch
eased past him and walked with as much dignity as she could muster into the kitchen. "I'm
Mitch Wallace. My parents own this place.
Would you like a cup of coffee?" She snapped
on the ceiling light as he followed her into the
room.

"Thanks, I would." He placed his headgear
and mitts on a kitchen chair and unzipped his
black leather jacket.

Acutely aware that he was watching her
every move, Mitch went to the percolator she
kept going constantly when she was writing (or
trying to write) and filled two thick white
mugs. Now that her initial fright was passing,

she was becoming embarrassingly aware of the blue towel wrapped loosely about her wet hair and the fluffy orange slippers matted with age on her feet. Just her luck that she had to meet the best-looking male she had seen in many moons at such a moment. Not that she was interested.

"Cream, sugar?" she asked, placing the mugs on the table.

"Black, thanks. It'll help keep me awake until I finish my appointed rounds." He grinned, the corners of his eyes crinkling, his lips raising slightly higher at one end in a way Mitch found devilishly appealing. "I live in a cabin upriver and I still have a few miles to go before I'm home."

He removed his jacket, hung it over the back of a chair, and sat down, still wearing the leather pants of his snowmobile suit, its bib and braces stretched over a broad, muscular chest.

This guy is terrific, Mitch thought as she took a chair opposite him and saw him clearly in the light of the hundred-watt bulb. *He could be the hero I've been looking for. Now, if he only has a mysterious past, has pulled off the daring capture of camp vandals . . .*

"What breed of dog is she?" Dan interrupted

her mental meanderings. He was patting Sadie again and the little dog was looking up at him with friendly interest. "I've never seen one quite like her. She resembles a red fox."

"She's a Nova Scotia duck-tolling retriever," Mitch said. "It's a relatively rare breed but distinctly Canadian. They were bred in Yarmouth, Nova Scotia to retrieve ducks and geese for hunters and attract waterfowl because they resemble a red fox."

"Hey, that's amazing!" he said, scratching Sadie's ears as she sat happily beside her new friend. "Have you had her long?"

"Four years," she said, warming to his apparently sincere interest in her beloved Sadie. "My parents own her mother. We've always had a least two tollers in our family as long as I can remember."

"Tollers. I guess that's a nickname for Nova Scotia duck-tolling retriever." He grinned. "It's a lot less cumbersome, isn't it, girl?" He addressed the last sentence to the little dog. She barked happily in reply and he laughed.

"As smart as you are pretty, aren't you?" He chuckled and Mitch felt her doubts about him dissolving. He was not only handsome, charming, and unassuming, but he genuinely liked Sadie and Sadie liked him.

"Do you patrol every day?" she asked, wrapping her fingers around her warm cup.

"Usually," he replied, settling back comfortably in his chair. "Although this is really only supposed to be a part-time job. It's dished out mostly to guys on social assistance who haven't worked for a while and are without a criminal record. Keeps them from becoming total idlers. I'm a plumber by trade. Just haven't been working at it lately except for the occasional job Brad lines up for me. Actually I would have thought he'd have asked me to open up this place for you when you called to say you were coming."

"I didn't notify Constable Stuart," she said. After her arrest she'd wanted no more contact with law enforcement officers, not even on an innocuous matter like opening up the family cottage. "I know most seasonal residents do advise him when they're getting ready to return. He has keys to most of the cabins and cottages and has always been terrific at getting water, electricity, and phone lines reconnected for us. But this time I decided not to bother him. I simply called a plumber in town who's a friend of my father's and also has a key to the cottage. He was great. When I arrived the place was warm, the water connected, and the phone line humming."

"Sounds like your decision to come here was a spur-of-the-moment one," he said, watching her closely.

"Sort of." Mitch was beginning to feel annoyed by his probing as she saw the bottom drop out of her glorious plan to make him the hero of her unborn novel. An unemployed plumber on social assistance who was given part-time security work to keep him from becoming bone-idle lazy was not what she'd been looking for in the way of a hero. Apparently all this character had going for him was drop-dead good looks and rampant charm.

"I can understand wanting to come here at any time," he said, looking around the cottage. "This place is as terrific inside as out."

"I do love it," she admitted, surprised at his appreciation of her beloved family hideaway. "But not everyone is turned on by what I'd call Seventies Wilderness Retro."

"Well, number me among the 'turned on.' " He grinned and she felt all her former annoyance with him vanish.

"Oreo?" she asked, opening a door and taking out a package of cookies.

"No, thanks," he said, getting up with a

scraping of his chair. "I prefer homemade cookies. Anyway, like Robert Frost once wrote, 'I have promises to keep, and miles to go before I sleep,' and I'd better get to it."

"Thanks for stopping," she said, placing her hands on the back of one of the hardwood chairs and watching as he put on his jacket. She liked the way his gray turtleneck tightened across his chest muscles as he thrust his arms into the sleeves. "In spite of my less-than-warm welcome, I do appreciate your concern."

"No problem. All a part of the service." He picked up his helmet and mitts and walked to the door, then turned back to her with his hand on the knob.

"Just one bit of advice," he said. "If I were you, I'd lock my doors when I took a shower at night. Anybody or anything might decide to drop in and they might not all be as affable as me."

"Anybody or *anything?*" she scoffed lightly. "Do you expect a rogue rabbit or a deadly deer to turn the latch and just sashay on in? They're about the only nonhuman creatures around here."

"Are you sure?" He opened the back door to look up into the clear night sky where stars sparkled like diamonds on black velvet. "Look up there and tell me you're positive we're the only thinking, scheming creatures in the universe. Just because we haven't mastered interplanetary travel yet, doesn't mean someone—or something—else hasn't."

"Are you trying to frighten me?" Mitch put her hands on her hips and faced him squarely. "And with visiting aliens? Give me a break!"

"I only want you to lock your doors at night," he said. "After seeing the look on your face when you found me in your kitchen in my helmet and suit, using the possibility of an alien invasion seemed appropriate. I can imagine how I must have looked in lamplight, and it obviously scared the daylights out of you."

"Well, thanks for trying to destroy my peace of mind," she said sarcastically, but inwardly burning with embarrassment to learn he had read her thoughts and fears so accurately. "I hope you don't use this type of scare tactic on any nervous little old ladies you might encounter on your rounds."

"Fortunately I don't know any nervous little old ladies who live at road's end in an isolated cottage in the dead of winter," he said, his eyes twinkling.

He was teasing her, baiting her, thoroughly

enjoying the give-and-take in their sparring. And so was she, she realized.

"Well, good," she shot back. "Otherwise I'm sure your stories would create a few heart attacks."

"But not for you," he said and turned away. "Remember to lock up after I leave."

Mitch watched from the kitchen window as he climbed aboard his snowmobile and, with a wave toward the kitchen window where she stood, drove away into the night.

An unemployed plumber on a snowmobile. Mitch threw up her hands in dismay. You couldn't get much farther from a mysterious hero on a white horse. She turned and padded back into the bathroom, Sadie at her heels.

Most of the steam had cleared from the mirror. She paused in front of it, pulled the towel from her head, and grimaced as her hair rooster-tailed free. Thank heaven she'd managed to keep it covered while Dan had been there, she thought, then wondered why she cared. If she'd learned anything from her involvement with Ken Clark, it was that men like him—handsome, charming men—were not to be trusted, depended upon, and most definitely not loved. Dan Jeffrey was only another shining example of the category.

She picked up a brush and began to whisk it through the one-length cap of her hair. When it hung neatly at her earlobes she paused and perused her reflection again. *Mitch,* she thought. What had become of Michelle with the soft, golden hair falling in waves about her shoulders, green eyes full of trust and concern? When had she metamorphosed into this trendy, uptown lady with a quick, careless comeback always on the tip of her tongue?

The question was rhetorical. She knew exactly when the change had begun. It had started on the day she had met reporter Ken Clark. She had just finished college. Hoping to build a career as a writer, she had taken a job in the mail room of the *National Mail,* one of Canada's leading daily newspapers.

Ken, a rising star among the reporting staff, had spotted her immediately. Soon he had had her promoted to his assistant, where she either took notes while he snapped pictures or, more commonly, reversed these positions. Unassuming, eager to please, and trusting, Michelle Wallace had been putty in the hands and plans of a charismatic, movie-star-handsome man like Ken Clark.

When he had decided she needed a new look, she had easily acquiesced. Her hair had been capped to one all-over, below-the-ears length, her pants and sweaters replaced by short-skirted suits, and her makeup, which had generally consisted of a dash of lipstick, changed to a slick, fashion-model paint job.

She grimaced at the memory as she reached for her toothbrush and squiggled a string of paste over it. She'd even had her teeth bonded and capped to please Ken. The more beautiful a female reporter was, the more information she could get out of almost any man she interviewed, he'd said. Sometimes they would even confide facts to an attractive woman that could move a story from being buried near the back of the newspaper to front-page headlines. When Mitch had tried protesting that such tactics weren't ethical, he'd merely shrugged.

"Hey, they're adults with brains. If they aren't smart enough to guard their tongues around something that heats up their blood, they aren't smart enough to be in the game."

As they'd continued to work together, he'd also changed her name to Mitch.

"Bright, snappy, with-it, and gender friendly if you ever need to use it as a byline in a story better accepted from a man," he'd explained.

Although the idea hadn't held much appeal for her, she'd agreed. The reason was simple.

By that time she was romantically involved with Ken and willing to do almost anything he asked to please him.

As she scrubbed at those expensive teeth, she had to admit she had, at first, enjoyed sharing Ken's fast-paced, on-the-edge lifestyle. Spurred on by his swashbuckling recklessness, a sense of adventure she had always possessed but never allowed to run free had burst into full gallop.

She'd enjoyed the adrenaline rush of chasing subjects across hotel lobbies, through airports, out of courtrooms, down dark alleys, and even along on the 401 in Ken's high-powered, far-from-paid-for red Corvette. She had soon realized that some of Ken's methods were not according to Hoyle, but, infatuated with him and telling herself he was only doing his job, she'd managed to ignore the fact. Until that night in the councilor's office.

At first she had been reluctant to be a party to a break-in. And when she'd learned he actually had a key to the office she'd felt her heart lurch. Rumors she had recently been hearing regarding Ken's association with the councilor's wife had suddenly leaped into the realm of distinct probability. Where else could he have gotten a key? But when she'd con-

fronted him with the idea, he'd denied it ve-
hemently.

"The woman's old enough to be my
mother!" he'd yelled. "Are you calling me
some kind of gigolo? Well, hey, that's just
great!"

Michelle had wilted in the face of his display
of self-righteous anger. It humiliated her now
to think how she'd apologized and even
begged him to take her along on the burglary
to prove she believed him, trusted him.

Trust! There was that word again. It made
her choke as she rinsed her mouth. What a fool
she'd been. And how much smarter she was
now. She'd definitely never trust another man
again, she told herself as she replaced her
toothbrush in its holder and screwed the cap
back on the tube of paste. Not in this lifetime.

She went into the bedroom, climbed into
bed, and snapped off the light. Sadie jumped
up to snuggle in beside her as she always did.

"An unemployed plumber on a snowmobile—
who needs a guy like that?" she asked the little
dog. "I just got rid of one man whose middle
name is trouble. I certainly don't need another."

Sadie only yawned a squeaky yawn and bur-
rowed noncommittally into the quilts.

That night, however, Michelle dreamed of twinkling blue eyes and silky black hair and broad shoulders . . . and an unemployed plumber on a snowmobile who quoted Robert Frost and pondered the mysteries of the universe.

She awoke the next morning to a beautifully calm, cloudless day. The thermometer outside the kitchen window informed her it was a mild −6 degrees C, balmy for northern New Brunswick in February. Humming "Someday My Prince Will Come" from *Snow White and the Seven Dwarfs,* she put coffee and water into the percolator and snapped on her computer.

"Today we will write chapter one," she told Sadie. "Today we will get a handle on this project."

By 10:00 she wasn't as confident. Tales of lost love, lost wealth, lost reputation all appeared briefly on the screen only to be fated for deletion moments later. None of them rang true or had the least hint of originality about them, she thought dismally, leaning back in her chair to stretch cramped muscles. The truth about the hermit of Hart's Hollow had to be much more intriguing than anything she could imagine. If only she could meet him!

Then she heard the drone of an approaching

snowmobile. She looked out the window beyond her computer and saw a machine headed
upriver, the midmorning sun glinting off its
black-enameled hood and windscreen. In front
of her cottage, it veered off the trail and followed the path Dan Jeffrey had made the previous evening into her backyard.

"We have a visitor, Sadie," she said.

She suspected it might be the camp patrol
officer but couldn't be certain; she hadn't been
able to get a good look at his snowmobile in
the darkness the previous evening.

She found herself to be correct when the
driver halted his machine near her back door
and pulled off his helmet. He looked every bit
as good as she remembered and she swung on
her chair to check her appearance in the old
chrome toaster on the counter beside her.
Mitch grimaced at her distorted reflection in its
age-crazed surface.

Well, at least she could see that her face was
clean and her hair was smoothly in place. Not
that it mattered. She wasn't out to attract Dan
Jeffery.

His knock at the door brought her to her feet.

"Good morning," he began when she opened
it, but before he could continue Sadie let out a

joyful bark and rushed past Mitch to greet her new friend.

"Hi, girl," he said and laughed. "It's nice to see you, too. Especially when you're not clamped onto my leg."

"She likes you," Mitch said and was glad she was wearing her favorite pink sweater and best-fitting jeans as he turned his attention from Sadie to her.

"You must have been downriver early," she continued quickly as she saw approval turn to undisguised appreciation and decided it was time to get back on track if she really wasn't interested in the man.

"I had to go to Geraldine's for supplies," he said, indicating a packsack fastened to the back of the snowmobile. "There's a big storm headed this way and I thought I'd better stock up."

"But at the moment, there's not a cloud in the sky and it's gorgeous," Mitch said, looking about at the dazzling white snow, dark green conifers, and cloudless blue sky. "Sadie and I are planning to do a little snowshoeing later on. Right now I'm about to take a break. Would you like to come in for coffee . . . and an Oreo?" The last was offered with a teasing smile.

"Just coffee, thanks," he said. "I've brought the snacks."

He returned to his snowmobile, rummaged in the packsack, then held up a plastic bag of Geraldine's molasses cookies. "Geraldine asked me to deliver these. I'm hoping you'll invite the delivery man to share."

"Oh, wow!" Mitch moved aside in the doorway and welcomed him with a sweeping bow. "Step right this way, sir."

Five minutes later they were seated at the kitchen table, steaming cups of coffee in hand, a plate of thick, cinnamon-brown cookies rapidly diminishing between them. Sadie lay contentedly beneath the table munching a couple of her special dog biscuits sent by Geraldine via Dan.

"Geraldine said you're writing a book," he said finally, indicating the computer by the window. "Fiction?"

"Yes." She sighed, leaning back in her chair. "But I can't seem to get started."

"That's the most difficult part," he said. "First attempt?"

"Not really," she said. "For the last three years I've worked as a reporter on the *National Mail.*"

"Really?" Dan straightened up in his chair,

his expression and tone hardening simultaneously. "A genuine ambulance-chasing, celebrity-dogging reporter?"

Paparazzi. Mitch could almost see the word racing across his mind with all its negative connotations in tow.

"I suppose I was," she admitted. "But as it turned out, I wasn't very good at it. So I decided to get out of the news business and came down here to find the peace I need to write my novel."

"It *is* peaceful," he replied, and Mitch was relieved as he leaned back in his chair, his tone moderating; his lips, however, remained hardened into a thin line and his eyes had lost all their friendliness. "Although, if you're not comfortable with being alone for long periods, it can be a little unsettling."

"Are we pretty much alone?" she asked, seeing an opportunity to guide the conversation around to a subject that was of intense interest to her.

"Except for the odd weekend party of snowmobilers."

"And the hermit up at Hart's Hollow," she said, watching his expression carefully.

"How could you possibly know about him?" Dan jerked ramrod straight in his chair and looked as if she'd just thrown a bucket of ice water over him.

"Geraldine told me," she said, startled. "What's the big deal? Is he a friend of yours or something?"

"Geraldine." He slumped back in his chair and slowly a wry grin relaxed his lips. "I might have guessed. The local newscaster, commentator, and talk-show host."

"Of course." Mitch was astonished at the acuteness of his knee-jerk reaction to her casual reference to the hermit. "Why? Where on earth else would I have heard about a local backwoods recluse? I only arrived here a couple of days ago. Is this resident Grizzly Adams a friend of yours?"

"We know each other," he said, avoiding her gaze as he arose. "I've got to be going. With this storm bearing down on us, I have a lot of work to do around my cabin. Thanks for the coffee."

His last words were civil but his relaxed affability had gone and Mitch instantly felt, for no reason she could pinpoint, as if she were about to lose something very important. She got up hastily and rounded the table to block his leaving.

"Thanks for the cookies. But really, there

can't be any great hurry. It's early yet, and—"

"And Mitch Wallace, girl reporter, wants to question me further about that poor old man upriver," he said as he thrust his arms angrily into the sleeves of his jacket, voice and eyes reflecting his annoyance. "I get the picture. You're planning to use the hermit as subject matter for some quick, sensationalist book that will hit the shelves in a matter of weeks, poorly edited and—"

"That's not my plan at all!" she exclaimed, startled by his (even if technically inaccurate) perceptiveness. "What makes you think something like that?"

"Then, tell me, why else would a Toronto reporter suddenly show up here in February?" He was glaring down at her with an anger she was finding difficult to understand. "This isn't exactly one of this season's hot spots!"

"I told you, to write a book!"

"About a hermit you didn't even know was living here when you made that decision? Come on, tell me something I can believe!" He yanked up his jacket's zipper, grabbed his mitts and helmet, and started for the back door.

"Okay, okay!" Mitch knew she had to get back into his good graces if she were to learn more about the hermit. "There was another reason. My boyfriend and I recently broke up! I couldn't bear to stay in the same city with him! Now are you satisfied?"

She swung away from him and pretended to feel much worse about Ken Clark than she did. When she heard him stop abruptly she squeezed crossed fingers until they hurt as she begged the Powers That Be to let him believe her and not be angry anymore.

"Hey, look, I'm sorry." His tone had softened considerably when he finally spoke and Mitch suppressed a sigh of relief. "I didn't know. Geraldine didn't tell me that part. I didn't mean to open up old wounds. I just was afraid you'd come here to bother a harmless old man who doesn't deserve to be hassled."

"You couldn't know," she said, fighting for a piteous little voice.

"Well, anyway, I'm sorry."

He turned and strode out of the cabin toward his snowmobile. Mitch shoved her feet into her boots, grabbed a jacket, and raced after him.

"But what *is* he like?" She ran to join him as he readied his snowmobile to leave.

"What do you mean, what's he like?" Dan paused, leaning forward on the handlebars, and squinted up at her in the sun. "I thought you were here to let a broken heart heal."

"I am," she said, suppressing the eagerness in her tone as best she could. "I plan to lose myself in my writing." Then she brought herself up to speed once more. "Is he tall, short, handsome, ugly, kind, nasty . . . what?" Mitch planted herself, arms akimbo, directly in front of his snowmobile. "Tell me or you'll have to make a permanent snow angel out of me with that machine before I'll let you go!"

"All right, all right." With a weary sigh, Dan swung his leg over the seat and sat down. "Man, your heart heals fast! He's tall and . . ." He paused.

"And, and?!" Mitch felt like shaking the words out of him.

"And just about the dirtiest human being on the face of the earth," he finished, reaching for his helmet. "I don't think he's had a bath or washed that long gray hair or beard in months, years maybe. Now, may I go?"

Mitch cocked her head and didn't move. "Are you telling the truth?"

"Would I lie to you?" The irresistible crooked grin surfaced and Mitch found herself again fighting its appeal.

"Maybe, if you thought it would get me off your back."

"So that's for you to decide, then, isn't it, Lois Lane?" He put on his helmet, started the motor, revved it a couple of times, backed his machine a few feet away, then dodged smoothly around her toward the river trail.

"These machines work great in reverse!" he yelled above the noise as he swung neatly past her.

Mitch ground her teeth and grabbed a handful of snow to fling after his out-of-range form.

"Well, I guess that's that," Mitch said to Sadie as the pair watched man and snowmobile disappear around a bend in the river. "Tomorrow we'll just have to set out to visit that hermit ourselves."

Chapter Three

The day dawned with an orange sun peeping over the treetops, then rising golden and unhindered into a clear blue sky. The tall pines that surrounded the cottage, lightly iced from a gentle snowfall during the night, glistened as if sprinkled with millions of diamond chips. Dan's snowmobile tracks had even been completely obliterated from the frozen river.

Mitch, in a forest-green snowsuit, gray toque, mitts, and mukluks stepped out onto the veranda carrying her snowshoes and took a deep breath of the cold, crisp air. Unable to restrain her joy in the perfection of the day, Sadie leaped past her down the steps and flung herself nose first into a fluffy drift.

"Nut!" Mitch laughed. "Enough fooling around already. Let's get to it."

She came down the steps and began to strap on her snowshoes. "Our mission today is to find the hermit and uncover his mysterious past. Dan Jeffrey's description just won't do. I have to see for myself."

Thoughts of the tall, good-looking camp patrol officer suddenly flooded back and her fingers slowed in fastening the buckles about her boots. Blue eyes twinkling with mischief flitted across her mind and she sighed. *Too bad,* she thought, straightening up. *He's attractive and kind of nice. Too bad I'm not about to let myself get involved again—now or ever.*

Five minutes later she and Sadie were plodding upriver, the little dog sometimes rushing ahead in fits of exuberance, sometimes trailing behind in her mistress's tracks to get a brief respite, sometimes trying to hitch a playful ride on the back of Mitch's snowshoes. Mitch laughed at her companion's antics and paused to draw in a deep breath of that wonderful, smog-free air.

"Do you know, Sadie, that this part of the province has the most pollution-free air in the Maritimes?" she asked. "There's not a single industrial complex for nearly a hundred miles and even then, nothing to cause major concern. I could get very comfortable living here."

At noon, feeling sure she was near the brook that led to Hart's Hollow, she decided to eat her lunch. She'd need to be at her best when she met the elusive hermit, and an empty stomach had never done that for her.

She left the river and made her way into the woods until she came to a stump protruding out of the snow. Using it as a chair, she sat down and opened her backpack. Inside were a thermos of coffee, a thick roast beef sandwich, three Oreos, a water bottle, and a plastic bag full of Sadie's gourmet dog treats. The little dog, ever alert, was instantly sitting at attention in front of her.

"Okay, okay," Mitch tossed her a biscuit and laughed at her perfect catch. "Not about to let one of those goodies disappear into a snow-drift, are you?"

As she unwrapped her sandwich she remembered how she had considered making another in case she met Dan. And almost instantly had decided against the idea. If their paths crossed he would likely be too annoyed with her for ignoring his advice about the hermit to share a snack.

As she settled to enjoy her lunch, memories

of another winter expedition up the river came to mind. She and her parents had spent one winter vacation at the cabin during her childhood and the three, with the family dog in tow, had snowshoed upriver on a day much like this.

Mitch recalled the fun her parents had had and how her father had actually burst into a version of his favorite love song, something about the hero being a carpenter, and would his lady marry him anyway?

Then her parents had laughed and explained to Mitch how appropriate that song had been to their situation when they had met and married. Their delight in the memory and each other had glistened in the beauty of that winter's day, Mitch recalled nostalgically, a little smile tipping her lips.

Suddenly she found herself thinking again of Dan the plumber, the affable, easy-on-the-eyes unemployed plumber. Quickly she gave herself a mental reprimand. Her parents' kind of relationship belonged to a time called then, when loving, trustworthy commitments still existed. This was now, a time when the only romance came from books and carpenters or plumbers did not live happily ever after with either ladies or self-sufficient reporters-turned-novelists.

She finished her lunch quickly and headed back to the river.

While she had been eating, a wind had arisen. The moment she stepped out onto the frozen river, it hit her with the shocking force of a hot shower suddenly turned cold. Swirling drifts were skimming across its surface, eddying over her snowshoe tracks to craftily obliterate them.

She frowned a little, then shrugged. What difference did it make? She didn't need her old trail to find her way back down the river. Probably it was just as well it was being wiped out. That way there would be nothing for Dan to follow if he did happen to be patrolling near her cottage.

She smiled. This thing with Dan and the hermit and herself was turning into an intriguing game and she was enjoying the challenge immensely.

An hour later, however, her enthusiasm was waning. She had started up two brooks, each of which she was certain must lead to Hart's Hollow. In both cases her quests had ended in alder thickets. The Hart's Hollow brook that she remembered as a child had flowed out of a lovely little valley and had been wide and deep enough to allow a canoe to sail up at least a half mile.

But, then, she told herself, that had been years ago. Things grow, branches and trees cluster in toward water, and memories become cloudy.

She paused and looked about. The wind was still rising, the cold intensifying. Clouds were sliding into place around the sun, ready to obscure it at a moment's notice. Sadie looked up questioningly at her mistress.

"Just a little further, babe," Mitch told her companion. "If the next brook doesn't look like it, we'll pack it in, I promise."

A half hour later she turned disappointedly toward home.

"That wasn't it either, Sadie," she said, and was startled at how cold the wind had become when she turned to face into it.

It was nearing 4:00, clouds had covered the sun, and snow blown free from the river's surface swirled and coiled in ghostly eddies up into the frosty air. Another increase in velocity and she'd be facing whiteout conditions, Mitch realized, feeling her level of concern rise.

"Come on, Sadie, let's move," she said, starting off at an enriched pace. "Darkness comes early at this time of year."

The wind flung hard bits of frozen snow into her face until she could see only a few feet in front of her. Her cheeks began to hurt.

"We'll have to go into the woods for shelter," she cried. "Come on, girl."

She had to go several yards into the trees to find sufficient protection Soon alder thickets and blowing snow blotted out the river. Traveling a course she believed was parallel to it, Mitch plodded steadily through the darkening day.

A half hour later she paused to catch her breath, disturbed to find that she was tiring. The wind at gale force in the evergreen canopy sounded like ocean surf in a hurricane.

"We'll go out to the river and check our bearings, Sadie," she said, trying to ignore the knot of fear starting to form in the pit of her stomach. "Then I'll know exactly where we are."

She turned to her left and for several minutes headed in what she believed to be the direction of the river. But slowly the truth became apparent. She and Sadie were lost!

The light of a cloud-darkened winter afternoon was starting to fade. Trees stood out tall, black, and menacing against a charcoal sky. The wind hissed through the naked arms of birches and maples and made the branches of the conifers creak and snap in the cold. Somewhere not far off a coyote broke into a nerve-rending howl. Exhausted, Mitch dropped against the trunk of a huge white pine and called Sadie. Then, with the little red dog clutched in her arms, she felt terror begin to coil its cold, slimy length about her heart.

"We'll be okay, Sadie," she told her companion. "We just have to stay calm."

But as nightfall blacked out her surroundings, Mitch found every terrible children's story she had ever heard or read beginning to slink across her imagination. An enchanted forest where trees came alive and loomed huge and threatening over human intruders. And wolves. Were there wolves in this forest? There were definitely coyotes. She'd just heard one. She could almost see their hungry yellow eyes peering out from behind windfalls, their attention pinned if not at first on her, most definitely on poor little Sadie.

And bears. What about bears? Was it true they hibernated all winter? Had there ever been cases of insomniac ones who roamed the February forest looking for a midwinter's snack?

Fear became a physical ache that started in the back of her neck and reached down to icy

feet and out into stiff, sore fingers. Her face
felt frozen into a brittle mask acutely sensitive
to the sting of the incessant barrage of snow
shards.

Minutes must have been stretching to hours,
she thought, judging from the descent of night.
How many hours she had no way of knowing.
She couldn't see her watch in the inky darkness
but she knew time was dragging by, marked
by ever-increasing discomfort and despair. The
wind gusted into an obscene shriek and Mitch
buried her face in the snow-hardened fur of
Sadie's neck to still her cry of terror. *We're
going to die,* she thought. *We're going to die
here alone in the cold and dark. And in the
spring, when the snow melts, they'll find us—
or what's left of us—just a little pile of bones,
if the animals haven't already dragged them
away.*

She thought about her parents and how they
would suffer when they learned her fate. "I've
caused them so much pain already, Sadie," she
told the little dog in her arms. "Now this!"

In the darkness she felt Sadie's whiskers
tickle her face. Then a warm tongue licked her
cheek.

"And you, darling Sadie," she whispered,

choking on a sob. "Look what I've done to you with my stupid quest for the hermit."

She thought of Dan and her earlier satisfaction in the fact that the snow had obliterated her snowshoe tracks. *How downright inane,* she thought. *I'd give anything right now to know there was a pristine set of tracks out there for him to follow.*

Suddenly Sadie tensed in her arms.

"What is it, girl?" she asked, raising her head. "What?"

A mutter erupted from the little dog's throat. The next instant she broke out of Mitch's arms and raced off into the darkness.

"Sadie!" Mitch tried to get to her feet to catch her dog but cold, cramped legs crumpled under her and she collapsed back against the tree.

"Sadie, don't leave me!" she choked. "Oh, please, don't leave me!"

She couldn't believe it. Her loyal little dog had deserted her. She looked up through the branches above her and saw a few stars beginning to glitter like hard, cold diamonds in the black heavens. *Please don't let me die here,* she begged. *All alone.*

Then she thought she saw a flash of light through the trees and above the swelling moans of the wind, another sound. An irregular roar. A motor? Mitch tried to get to her feet once again but again cramped and half frozen, she failed.

Please, please! she silently prayed. *I promise if I get out of this mess, I'll never try to find the hermit again!*

The light bouncing through the trees grew brighter, the up-and-down motor sounds nearer. Mitch squeezed her eyes shut tight and prayed.

Suddenly something frozen and furry bounded into her arms.

"Sadie!" she cried.

Seconds later Dan Jeffrey pulled up on his snowmobile.

"So you went looking for the hermit after all? After I specifically asked you to leave him alone!" His voice in the blackness was outraged. "I should leave you here, you stubborn heedless newshound! Anyone who can't respect another person's privacy any more than you do doesn't deserve compassion!"

Chapter Four

Mitch lay propped up on pillows on the couch in the living room of her cottage, swathed in quilts, a cup of chicken soup clutched in her reddened hands. Through the archway she could see the kitchen and Dan wearing jeans and a black turtleneck vigorously toweling Sadie dry. Her frozen outerwear was draped over chairs to thaw and dry. His snowmobile clothing lay crumpled in a pile near the back door.

It was the first time she had seen Dan without his snowmobile suit covering most of his body. Now she took a good, hard look while he was busy caring for Sadie. In old, naturally faded jeans that in spite of their age fit very well and a black turtleneck that revealed the muscular curves of his upper body, Dan Jeffrey could have passed as a professional athlete or a movie heartthrob. And to top it off, he'd just saved her life. He and Sadie.

I don't need this, she thought ruefully. *Not in my weakened and vulnerable state. Thank heaven he's furious with me.*

He finished drying the exhausted little dog, picked her up, and carried her into the living room. There he deposited her gently on the couch with Mitch.

"She's quite a dog," he said admiringly, rubbing Sadie's head affectionately before he straightened up. "I'd never have found you if she hadn't come for me."

"I realize that," Mitch said, hugging her close. "But I also realize you were probably out looking for me in this awful night. Otherwise, you wouldn't have been there for Sadie to find. Why?"

He sank down into a chair opposite her and she realized he looked tired, more tired than she would have believed a man of his vitality could look. She owed him, she decided. Big time.

"I was on my way home," he said, stretching out long, sock-footed legs and running a hand through his thick black hair. "And I saw this place in darkness, your Jeep in the yard. The two facts didn't compute. Then I remembered your noncommittal response to my suggestion that you abandon the idea of finding the hermit." He shrugged. "The rest was elementary, my dear Watson."

"Thanks, Holmes." She smiled as she saw his anger lessening. "Your deductions were excellent and most timely."

"I want more than thanks from you." He rose and reached down to take the empty soup cup from her hands. His fingers, the hard callused fingers of a man who worked with his hands, closed over hers, and penetrating blue eyes locked her gaze.

Mitch felt her heart skip a beat and gossamer wings flutter in her stomach. He was so handsome, so charming, and he'd just saved her life. What could she refuse him?

Slowly he dropped on his haunches beside the couch, his hands still over hers on the cup. "I want . . ."

"Yes?" Mitch felt her breath catch in her throat, her heart rate triple.

"I want you to promise never, never again to try to find the hermit."

"Oh, for heaven's sake!" Mitch pulled her hands away, leaving the empty cup in his.

"What?" He looked puzzled by her response. "What did you think I was going to say?"

"Nothing, nothing." Mitch concentrated on pulling a snag from Sadie's coat and hoped the blush she felt gushing over her face wasn't obvious.

"Oh, right!" Dan leaped to his feet and headed for the kitchen as realization dawned over him. "As if I'd take advantage of the situation! Man, but you must have a high opinion of me!"

He picked up the empty chicken soup can and flung it into the garbage with such a force it made Sadie flinch. Then he pulled open a cupboard door and began riffling through its contents, shoving spices, boxes, and jars noisily aside.

"Dan, I'm sorry." Mitch turned on the couch to look at him, realizing the sincerity in his anger. "I just thought . . . well, I guess I'm accustomed to big-city guys and their . . . intentions."

He stopped his rampage of the cupboards and turned to her.

"Yeah, well, maybe I jumped to a conclusion too fast, too. Let's just chalk it up to a comedy of errors and move on." He returned to his search.

"I was going to say no anyway."

"What?" He turned again from the cupboards.

"I was going to say no," she repeated, a trifle embarrassed. "Just for your information."

"Well . . . good." The hint of amusement in his voice sent a hot blush rushing up her cheeks. "Then perhaps a good, hearty slap in the jowls to impress the point?"

Leaving Mitch fuming, he went back to searching the shelves.

"What *are* you looking for?" she asked in an effort to change the subject permanently. "There's no need to mess everything up. I'll tell you where to find whatever it is."

"Matches," he said, peering back into the old cupboard's shadowy depths. "I'm going to light a fire in the fireplace. Electric heat is okay but you and Sadie need the warmth of a good wood fire right now."

"You can't," she said, settling back in her quilts.

"What?! Don't tell me you haven't got any matches?"

"No," she said, calmly rubbing Sadie's ears. "No flue. Dad blocks off the chimney on the roof each fall when he and Mom leave to keep birds and squirrels out."

"That's just great!" Dan's voice reflected his exasperation. "What would you do in a power outage? You've got no emergency source of heat whatsoever. Not even a gas range for cooking!" He indicated the new electric range.

"Dad didn't expect to use this place this winter," she said absently, tiredly. "It isn't a major problem; if I do lose electric power, I'll just pack up and move in with Geraldine."

"And leave your undrained pipes to freeze and burst? Have you thought about that?" His annoyance at her fecklessness bubbled over.

"Oh, I forgot!" Her absolute exhaustion surfaced in an inability to deal with even the smallest problem. "You're an unemployed plumber! Well, if the need ever arises, you can rest assured I'll let you drain my pipes!"

"Thanks." Dan looked as if she had just administered the slap he had joked about minutes before. He turned to the stove to remove the soup pot from a back burner.

Mitch couldn't believe what she had said. The man had saved her life and she had proceeded to mock him. And all he'd been doing was showing concern for her welfare.

"Dan, I'm sorry."

"Yeah, okay." He put the empty pot in the sink, rinsed, it, then turned back to her, no evidence of anger in his expression. "We're both bone tired. It's time we got some sleep. You'd better climb into your bed while your eyes are still open. I'll borrow one of those quilts you've got there and sleep on the couch. It's too late and I'm too bushed to go home."

"Of course you can't leave!" Mitch was instantly scrambling to her feet. "It's drifting. In fact"—she glanced toward a window to indicate the snow buffeting it—"it's whiteout conditions.

"And you don't have to sleep on the couch. My parents' bedroom is empty. Use it . . . please."

"Thanks," he said, snapping off the kitchen light. "Right now the idea of a warm bed is my concept of heaven. If you'll just point the way . . ."

"I'll show you." Mitch gathered up her cluster of quilts and headed for a hallway leading from the right side of the room. "This cottage has only two bedrooms, one on each side of this little hallway. The bathroom is at the end."

She pushed open a door on her left and snapped on a lamp. "I hope you'll be comfortable here."

A spacious room dominated by a large, quilt-covered four-poster bed came into view. A massive matching oak dresser sat in one corner beside a window that looked out across the snow-covered lawn to the river. In the soft tungsten lighting, with snow hissing at the windows and a gale whistling about the snug little cottage, the room was an oasis of warmth and security.

"This is great," he said, walking past her.

Then he paused and turned to look back at her as she stood framed in the doorway, clutching her quilts in front of her. "You're sure your parents won't mind?"

"Subletting their room to the man who just saved the life of their only child? I think not!" Mitch was indignant.

"Hey, don't get hostile again!" He came to stand in front of her, his tall form casting a long shadow over her in the lamplight. "Even if you are kind of attractive when you are."

"Kind of?" She struggled to stay casually neck-and-neck with his teasing tone but her heart had already taken the bit in its teeth and was racing far ahead.

"Well, okay. Maybe a real knock out." He reached out and ran his knuckles gently down her cheek.

Abruptly he turned and headed for the bed, pulling his sweater over his head as he went. "I'll see you at breakfast."

Mitch was awakened the next morning by a knocking at her front door. Only vaguely aware of the shower running, she stumbled groggily from her bed, wrapped herself in her robe, shoved her feet into slippers, and padded to answer it.

She was surprised to find Constable Bradley Stuart standing on her veranda. He was in uniform, his patrol jeep parked in the dooryard behind her Tracker.

"Good morning, Constable." She pushed tangled hair back with one hand and stifled a yawn with the other. "Come in. What brings you out here so early?"

"Good morning, Miss Wallace." He accepted her offer and stepped in out of a fine, bright winter's morning to pat a tail-wagging Sadie and smile at her mistress. "I'm looking for the camp patrol officer. You haven't seen D-Dan Jeffrey lately, have you? I haven't been able to contact him at his cabin since late yesterday. Then I saw his snowmobile parked in your drive and—"

As if on cue, Dan emerged from the steamy

bathroom, wearing only his jeans, a towel draped over his broad, bare shoulders. Mitch couldn't say which of the two men appeared more astonished.

"Hello, Brad." Dan was the first to speak.

"I got lost snowshoeing yesterday," she heard herself blurting out rapidly. "Dan . . . Mr. Jeffrey found Sadie and me and brought us home. And since it was too late and cold for him to go to his own place, he stayed in my parents' room. And I stayed in my room . . . and . . . Oh, for Pete's sake, I can't believe I'm doing this!" She caught at her hair with both hands in total exasperation.

"There's no need to explain." Constable Stuart was grinning. "I've known Dan quite a while. He can be a colossal pain in the neck but he's a gentleman." He looked over at Dan and shrugged.

"Thanks, buddy." Dan gave his friend an amused glance, then headed for the kitchen. "Is there any coffee?"

"I'll make it." Mitch swung away from them with a twitch of her head. "You two visit. I'm sure you'll want to tell the constable how my getting lost was all my fault, how you warned me against trying to find the hermit—"

"The hermit up at Hart's Hollow?" Brad

Stuart stopped short as he was about to take a chair near the fireplace. "You were looking for the hermit when you got lost?"

"Now don't you start on me, Constable," Mitch continued the conversation through the archway as she poured water into the coffee-maker. "Everyone around here keeps warning me against him. Unless you can offer irrefutable proof that he's a mass murderer, I won't listen to a word."

She measured coffee and watched furtively as the two men exchanged looks.

"Well, I can't do that," the mountie replied slowly. "But I can tell you he's a man who doesn't want to be disturbed, whose earned a little peace and—"

"Ah-ha!" Mitch bounded back into the living room and plunked herself down on the couch beside Dan, facing the officer. "A man with a sad or dubious past, a man hiding from a life that has left him wounded, a man of mystery—"

"I told you she was a writer," Dan interrupted with a tortured look of exasperation. "A few hundred years ago she would have put the Brothers Grimm out of business. I've already told her he's nothing but a dirty old bum who hasn't had a bath in so long you can smell him a mile away but still she insists on romanticizing him. Maybe if you tell her, she'll believe you. Everyone believes a mountie."

"Okay, tell me, Mountie." Mitch curled up in the corner of the couch farthest from Dan, pulled her feet up under her, and folded her arms stubbornly across her chest. "Tell me the whole truth about the hermit of Hart's Hollow."

"Well, the last time I saw him, he did have long gray hair and a beard," he said slowly, looking at Dan. "And he did appear . . . unkempt. As to being dirty, I really couldn't say—"

"Well, I can," Dan broke in. "I was there, remember? And, believe me, he smelled worse than any skunk I've ever encountered. Pretty romantic type of guy, right?" he finished sarcastically, looking at Mitch.

"I'm still not convinced." Mitch arose blithely and sauntered into the kitchen to check the coffee. "And since this was still a free country the last time I checked, I see no reason why I should abandon my quest."

She fancied she could hear Dan grinding his teeth behind her.

A half hour later Constable Stuart left and Mitch went into the bathroom to shower. Dan was frying bacon and eggs in the kitchen and playing fetch with Sadie and her beloved tennis ball. He could be one of the most exasperating men she'd ever met, she decided as she turned on the water and stepped into the warm, reviving flow, but he was also one of the bravest and most caring. He had risked his own life the previous night to find her. Surely no one was required to take such a chance for a job she felt reasonably certain paid minimum wage.

Maybe, in the spring when she returned to Toronto, she could convince him to go with her. Her father, with his connections in the building trade, could find him a job as a plumber. Surely that would be better than living on social assistance once the summer people returned to their cottages and cabins and the patrol would no longer be needed.

Twenty minutes later she returned to the kitchen in jeans and a blue turtleneck to find a plate of bacon, eggs, and toast ready for her. Dan was seated on a chair by the door, putting on his boots.

"You're leaving?" she asked and was surprised at the feeling of disappointment that came over her.

"Not just yet," he said, standing up and

reaching for his jacket. "First I'm going to get that flue functional. You never know when you might need to use it. Especially if that predicted storm hits in full force."

"If it will make you feel better." Mitch sighed and sat down at the table. "Hey, this looks great," she said, her enthusiasm returning as she looked at the breakfast plate complete with orange slice garnish. "You rescue maidens in distress, you fix chimneys, and now I discover you can cook." She braced her elbows on the table, cupped her chin in her hands, and said seriously, "Marry me."

He looked up from zippering his jacket and met her teasing gaze.

"Don't forget to ask me again when we're better acquainted," he said. "For now, I'll take an option on first refusal."

He turned and went out with Sadie leaping joyfully along beside him. Mitch was left speechless, not even the hint of an appropriate comeback in her mind.

"Be careful up there," Mitch called fifteen minutes later. Dressed in boots and snowsuit, she stood in a thigh-deep drift watching Dan on the cottage roof fastening screening over the newly opened flue.

"This will keep the little forest critters out and sparks in," he said, stepping back to admire his handiwork. "Now you can safely light a fire in—!"

His boots had slipped. With a yelp of surprise and an unsuccessful scrambling attempt to save himself, he toppled toward the edge of the roof of the single-story structure.

"I'll catch you!" Hindered by soft, deep snow Mitch lumbered clumsily forward, arms outstretched. She managed to get below the eave just as he tumbled over its edge.

Technically, she thought later, *I did catch him. The fact that he knocked me off my feet and nearly unconscious was secondary.*

At the time, however, it all happened so fast she didn't have a chance to analyze the situation. Dan's weight landed intact in her outstretched arms. It sent her backward into a drift with the force of a pile driver. For a moment, submerged in snow, her breath all but gone, she could only lie still and gasp.

"Good heavens! Mitch, Mitch! Speak to me! Are you all right?"

Dan was looming over her, wildly brushing snow from her face, his expression one of utter horror.

"I-I'm okay," she finally managed to gasp as he pulled her to her feet. "Really."

"I thought . . . man, you scared me! What made you think you could catch someone a good fifty pounds heavier than yourself? I could have hurt you!"

"Okay, okay!" she yelled back.

Their breath coming in gasps of mist in the frosty air, both suddenly stopped in mid-sentence. For a moment angry blue eyes met outraged green ones. Then, slowly, animosity crumpled into confusion. Then it melted into pure astonishment. Transfixed by the moment they stood stock still, galvanized by amazement.

Oh, my! Mitch thought, feeling a deliciously heady sensation wash over her. *Oh, my!*

When he leaned forward to take her into his arms, she was waiting, her lips turned up to him. As he kissed her lightly, tentatively, then deeply with confidence, Mitch felt her heart burst into song, her soul erupt into fireworks. She wouldn't have been surprised if the snow around them suddenly melted and spring blossoms sprouted on the old lilac bushes beside the front porch. No one, no one, not Ken Clark, not anyone had ever had that kind of effect on her.

When he finally, gently released her she could only stare at him, her eyes round with wonder.

"Well . . ." He exhaled.

"Well . . ." she breathed tonelessly.

"Ah, man, what am I doing?" Dan Jeffrey seemed to give himself a mental shake. Abruptly he released her and backed away.

"What . . . ?" Mitch was wide-eyed with surprise. "What?"

"Look, I shouldn't have done that." He brushed snow from the palms of his mitts. "I'm sorry, okay?"

Within seconds it seemed, he'd pulled on his helmet, climbed aboard his snowmobile, and, with a gunning of the motor, had driven away.

Sadie watched him drive out of sight, then barked sharply.

"I don't know, girl." Mitch grimaced as she started toward the veranda. "I don't know when he'll be back. Or if, for that matter. Or even if what I think happened just now really did or if it was simply a figment of imagination from a mind and body with every ounce of oxygen knocked out of it. Ouch!"

Hurting all the way, she went gingerly up the steps. She'd light a fire in the fireplace, make a fresh pot of coffee, and spend the rest of the day writing, she decided. She needed time to recuperate physically and emotionally from Dan Jeffrey.

Chapter Five

Twenty minutes later, settled comfortably on the couch, notepad and pencil on her lap, Mitch sat staring at the blank sheet of paper in front of her. Then absently, a shadow of a smile tipping her lips, she began to doodle. Wistfully she intertwined Dan's name or initials with her name or initials in a way she had not done since her first big crush in junior high.

Good heavens! She stopped and frowned down at the ornate scrawls. Hadn't four years of university and three years as a city reporter on a national newspaper made her any more sophisticated than this? But then the memory of his eyes, his voice, his kiss flooded back and unplanned roses blossomed in her heart. *Back on track,* she told herself. *I have to get back on track and figure out a way to meet the hermit. Dan Jeffrey, I'm putting you on hold.*

But it wasn't until after she had eaten her supper and was putting away the dishes that the answer came to her in a flash of inspiration.

"If Mitch can't go to the hermit, then the hermit must come to Mitch," she cried, turning to Sadie and hugging the little dog, delighted with her idea. "The next time Dan Jeffrey visits, we'll just convince him to get that mysterious recluse to come and visit us!"

She strolled slowly into the living room, hands clasped behind her back. "I'll just have to find some way to make Dan realize what a good idea it is."

Sadie, still sitting in the kitchen, barked in reply.

"Oh, I see." She turned back to the little dog and planted her hands on her hips. "You're wondering what makes me so sure Dan *will* come back. Well, I'm pretty sure he likes me . . . quite a lot. You were there when he fell off the roof. You saw what happened."

Sadie cocked her head and whined.

"Well, yes, I did enjoy it," she admitted. "But you know the deal. We are not, repeat, are not going to get involved. If Ken Clark taught me anything, it was not to trust anyone except my parents and you. Now—" She curled up cross-legged, yoga fashion, in an armchair. "To devise a plan to convince Dan to bring the hermit here."

The next morning she was showered, dressed, and had breakfasted on toast, juice, coffee, and cereal by 8:00. Then she took some of her mother's recipe books from a kitchen drawer and sat down at the table to peruse them.

"Peanut butter dreams, chocolate chip supremes, hermits—how appropriate!" She pursed her lips and frowned. "What's your opinion, Sadie? Do you think mouth-watering little goodies of sugar, flour, eggs, etc., called for some mysterious reason 'hermits,' might be sufficiently tantalizing and creative to convince Dan to bring the real hermit for a visit?"

Sadie gave her usual answering bark, then grew alert, ears cocked, listening. Mitch listened, too, and a moment later heard a vehicle coming down the road. She arose and got to the window just in time to see a red Corvette skid to a stop beside her Tracker. She gasped as the driver emerged.

What is he doing here? she thought, trying

to gather her reeling senses. *Ken Clark belongs in Toronto, should be in Toronto.*

The tall, broad-shouldered young man stood looking about for a few seconds, then ran fingers through artificially sun-streaked blond hair and started toward the cabin. His black leather jacket hung open to reveal a rib-knit tan turtleneck and perfectly fitted designer jeans.

Mitch waited until he knocked to go to the door. She'd thought of pretending she wasn't at home but Sadie had already barked and the Tracker was in the yard. Anyway, she consoled herself as she reached for the knob, she couldn't continue to run from her past. This would give her an opportunity to face up to it once and for all and maybe bring it to some sort of closure.

"Hello, Ken." She pulled open the door. "This is a surprise. I haven't seen you since . . ." She put a finger to her temple in a pretence of trying to remember. ". . . since you deserted me in that councilor's office."

"And I've missed you, babe. Why else do you think I've come all this way?"

He was as smooth and handsome as ever, as confident as if nothing had ever gone wrong between them.

"I really have no idea," she said, staring at

him coldly and pleased to discover the fascination he'd once held for her was completely gone. "But I'm absolutely certain it had nothing whatsoever to do with me."

"Come on, Mitch, honey." He brought what had once been, for her, his devastating charm into play and smiled, revealing perfect white teeth. "Let me come in and explain. It's freezing out here."

He started to step into the cabin but Sadie stopped him with a snarl.

"Still got that wicked little witch, I see," he said, pausing. "Call her off, Mitch. I don't want her ruining my pants."

"It's okay . . . for now, Sadie." Mitch moved aside to let the man enter. "But if he does or says anything I don't like, feel free to tear those Calvin Kleins right off their moorings."

"Bitter, bitter." Ken grinned and wagged a teasing finger under her nose. "And all because of one little incident."

"That 'little incident,' as you choose to call it, cost me my job and not only my reputation as a journalist but very nearly my father's as a contractor as well. Dad could have lost all his city works contracts, thanks to you!" She grabbed his hand and angrily pulled it out of her face. "So just get the point, Ken, and get out!"

"Okay, okay." He crossed the room and dropped into one of the worn old armchairs by the fireplace. "Quaint," he said, looking around. "You've really gone back to basics, haven't you, Mitch? I wouldn't have believed it if I hadn't seen it. I thought you were permanently Yonge Street chic."

He ran his gaze over her slender form in jeans, plaid flannel shirt, gray woolen socks, and leather moccasins. "I sort of like it."

"And I sort of couldn't care less!" Mitch went to stand in front of him, arms crossed, green eyes glinting emerald fire down on him. "Get to the point!"

"Sure, sure." He shrugged. "Business as usual if that's what you want. Maybe you caught my front-page piece on D. J. Carson's disappearance?"

"Vaguely," Mitch replied, trying to recall the article she had glanced at briefly in Geraldine's store two days ago.

"Well, I'm on special assignment from the paper to find him," he said, smug satisfaction mirrored in his face.

"Then why are you here?" she asked. "He vanished from Toronto, didn't he? He could be anywhere. And this place has every reason to top the list of least likely."

"Ah-ha!" Ken Clark was triumphant. "That's where my excellent skills as an investigator come in. I researched his past and learned his best friend is a guy he went to university with, one Bradley Stuart."

"The local RCMP officer." Mitch breathed in surprise.

"Right. And I also learned that D. J. often makes unpublicized trips down here to visit him. So I thought what better place for a guy hiding from his obligations to go. So here I am."

"Hiding from his obligations? What do you mean? I thought there were strong reasons to believe he was kidnapped."

"Kidnapped?" Ken sneered. "I'd like to see who'd try. The guy's built like an Olympic athlete and is twice as tough. No, he ran away, pure and simple. His agent had booked him into a big publicity tour. D. J. refused to honor it and split. Apparently the guy has a deepseated aversion to the press, a real phobia, I've been told. Now unless someone finds him, his publisher and promotion agency are going to be out one large chunk of change."

"So you decided to save them all that heartache," Mitch said sarcastically, rocking back on her heels and crossing her arms on her chest. "And, for a sizable reward—which, if I remember correctly, is also a nice chunk of change—set out to find him."

"Hey, I'm a crack investigative reporter," he said, getting up to stand so close in front of her she caught the scent of his expensive aftershave . . . and remembered. "My work will benefit everybody, including the *National Mail.* I could even get a promotion to assistant editor, although I'm not sure I want it just yet. I'd rather be out in the field making a name for myself. And you could still be part of that, baby. Help me on this one, then come back to Toronto with me. We had a great partnership once. We can again."

He reached out to take her into his arms but Mitch neatly stepped aside.

"A real partner doesn't leave his other half in trouble!" she barked. "A real partner is dependable, trustworthy! But you wouldn't know anything about that, would you?"

She started to turn away but he grabbed her, spun her about, and wrenched her into his arms. Before Mitch could stop him, his mouth covered hers in a hard, cold kiss.

"Stop it!" With a supreme effort Mitch

turned her face away from his and pushed free. Once she had found his kisses enjoyable, but now she found them purely repugnant. "Get out!"

"Hey, cool down. No need to go ballistic." He accepted her rebuff as easily as if she'd just refused him the loan of her car, and stepped away. "If love has died, that's okay with me. We can still work together. All I want you to do is tell me if you've seen anyone around here who might possibly be D. J. Carson. I asked that crazy old lady at the convenience store but she said the only writer around here was a woman. Then I remembered your folks had a summer place near here, put two and two together, and here I am. Mitch . . ." His tone became soft and conciliatory. "I've really missed you. I wanted to come forward when you were arrested but I just couldn't see what good it would do. It would only have mucked up my career, too. But if you were to help me out on this story, I'm sure I could convince the editor-in-chief to rehire you. Come on, what do you say? You know the people around here. They'll talk to you. If D. J. Carson is hiding out in the vicinity, someone's bound to know."

"Why don't you go ask his mountie friend?" she said, brushing away and moving across the room to look out the window at Dan's snow-mobile tracks on the river ice. "Mounties never lie."

"I did." He sighed in exasperation. "He said D. J. Carson definitely isn't staying with him."

"So there you have it." Mitch swung back to face him. "He isn't staying here."

"Not with the mountie," he corrected her. "That's not to say he isn't hiding out some-where in the area. I'm sure he made some friends among the locals during his visits. Any one of them could be covering for him. That's where you come in. They'll talk to you, confide in you."

"And I'll consequently betray their trust." Mitch shook her head, surprised that she could still be amazed at the depths to which Ken Clark would sink for a story. "I think not, Ken. These people have known my family and me for years. I'm not about to use them. Further-more, I wouldn't know this D. J. Carson if I fell over him. I've never seen his picture."

"There aren't any around," Ken said, look-ing around the room distractedly. "Believe me, I've checked. He avoids the paparazzi like the plague—prefers anonymity to fame. A good picture of D. J. Carson would probably be worth a fair bit. He won't even allow one on the dust jackets of his books. From what I've heard, though, he's kind of good-looking, tall, well-built, with blond hair he usually wears shoulder length or longer and a moustache. Help me on this one, babe, and you can come back to Toronto in style, all past sins forgiven. You can't really want to spend the rest of the winter here in this dump."

"Get out, Ken." Mitch planted her feet firmly, crossed her arms on her chest, and nodded toward the door. "My parents and I happen to love this dump, as you call it, and right now I wouldn't trade it for the most fabulous penthouse in Toronto!"

"Okay, okay. Just help me on this one for old times' sake? I'm a bit behind on the 'Vette's payments and my landlord is hollering for last month's rent. I need the reward money to get me back on track . . . back to putting Councilor Giverson away. You know how important that is."

"On that we agree." She walked over to the door and held it open for him. "But this time you're on your own. That crusade of yours cost me my job, but worst of all, it could have ruined my father's business. I won't play Robin to your Batman anymore, Ken!"

"Come on, babe." He ignored her dismissive

gesture and remained where he was. "You know you'd do anything to be back at the paper and, believe me, I can make it happen. You and I are a lot alike, sweetie, even if you don't want to admit it. I know what makes you tick and what makes your engine rev, and it's not a shack in the backwoods with a dog and a computer for company."

"You couldn't be more wrong, *sweetie!*" she snapped. Her heart was pounding with outrage. "You see, I've discovered I'm not at all like you and I'm glad. Now do me one last huge favor and get out before I turn my wicked little witch loose on you!"

Twenty minutes later, with Ken Clark gone and her heart slowed to a normal pace, Mitch returned to the cookbooks. The memory of her former partner slipping and scrambling over ice and snow toward his unaffordable car with Sadie barking and nipping at his heels made her smile.

"Hermits," she decided, feeling more light hearted than she had in days as she looked over the recipes. " 'Spicy brown sugar drop cookies with raisins and nuts that melt in your mouth,' " she read the book's description. "Hmmm . . . tasty and hopefully evocative for Dan Jeffrey."

She arose and began to assemble utensils and ingredients on the counter, humming snatches of "Annie's Song." She wasn't thinking about Ken Clark when she sang the romantic words.

Chapter Six

"Mitch, where are you? Mitch, are you okay?"

Dan's yell yanked her out of the story and made her glance toward the kitchen.

"Oh, no!" she cried, leaping to her feet and flinging the book aside.

A thick dark cloud was billowing through the archway into the living room.

"Mitch! Answer me! Where are you?"

Dan's voice told her he was already in the smoke-filled room.

"I'm okay," she called back, waving a hand in front of her and advancing into the cloud. "It's only my cookies burning. I forgot them in the oven."

Through smoke-stung eyes she saw Dan drop open the oven door to let out a charcoal puff. Choking, he grabbed the tray inside with his snowmobile mitt and, shedding black circles that had once been hermits, strode to the back door to fling the remains out onto the snow. Sadie, in true retriever fashion, raced after them.

Still coughing, Dan left the back door open and returned to open the window above the sink. Then he looked at Mitch.

"What *were* you doing?" he asked as the draft between window and door began to clear the fog. "When I came up on your back step and, through the window in the door, saw the kitchen full of smoke, I thought the cottage was on fire."

"I was . . . making cookies," she said, looking at the bits of charcoal lying in a trail from oven to back door and out into the snow. "You said you liked homemade ones so I thought I'd whip up a batch."

"You were making cookies . . . for me?" Dan's eyes widened in surprise. "Hey, that's incredibly sweet."

"Oh, shut up!" Mitch felt herself suddenly bursting with anger and embarrassment. "It was only because you saved my life the other day. Don't go getting any romantic notions about it!"

"Hey, no way. Not me." Dan threw up his hands and backed off a step. "Cookies are a great way to say thanks for saving your heedless hide. But next time you don't take my advice and I pull you out of the resulting life-threatening situation, I'll expect a full-course dinner."

"Don't hold your breath, chum," she snapped.

"Okay," he agreed easily. "But I won't put my search-and-rescue persona in mothballs, either."

"Speaking of life-threatening situations . . ." She couldn't help taking advantage of the opportunity. "Yesterday, when you fell off the roof, did you kiss me or did lack of oxygen make me hallucinate?"

"I did," he admitted.

"And then you ran away, almost as if you were sorry it had happened. Why?"

"I wasn't sorry," he said flatly. "I definitely wasn't sorry. I was scared."

"Scared? Of what?"

"Of starting something I wasn't sure I could . . . we could finish," he said. "You're a big-city reporter, I'm a country plumber. Somehow I couldn't see that combination blending."

"And now?"

"Now I don't know. You're a puzzle, Mitch Wallace. Tucking me into bed in your parents' room, risking your neck in a courageous if misguided attempt to save me from injury when I slipped off your roof, and now this cookie thing. None of the above compute with my perception of the paparazzi."

"I'd hardly call what I did tucking you into bed." She turned away to gaze out the open door. "And as for the roof thing, I only did what anyone would for a person in danger."

"Not anyone. Most definitely not a true paparazzi." His tone became bitter. "A true paparazzi would have been rushing off for a camera to capture the moment no matter how devastating for the person involved."

"Suppose you tell me why you have this deep and abiding hatred for the press." Mitch turned back to face him squarely and crossed her arms on her chest. "There has to be a specific reason. Generalities don't cause an animosity as intense as yours."

"Okay, okay, I'll tell you." He walked over to the open door, caught the top of its frame in one hand, and stood staring out into the sheltering pines. "Three years ago my niece and I were at the airport in Toronto. Mindy was only six and she and I were on our way to visit that big amusement park, Canada's Wonderland. We were crossing the parking lot when a guy in a red Corvette, hot on the trail of some celebrity, careened across in front of us. He missed Mindy by inches. Needless to say, it scared the poor kid senseless. It took hours for me to calm her down. The incident all but ruined our three-day vacation."

Ken! Mitch stifled a gasp and was glad his back was turned to her. Otherwise, she was certain her shock and chagrin would have been easily seen in her face. She remembered that day. Ken had left her at the office to enter a story into the computer and rushed off in pursuit of Tom Cruise. One of his sources had tipped him off that the movie star would be arriving at Pearson International that afternoon, and he didn't want to miss the chance to get a few candid shots.

Mitch had wanted desperately to go along. After all, how often did one get a chance to see Tom Cruise in person? Now she was eternally grateful Ken had refused to take her with him.

"Dan, I'm sorry," she said softly. "That must

have been a horrible experience for you and Mindy. But how do you know the driver of that car was paparazzi?"

"When he screeched to a stop, you can bet I was right there. I pulled him out of that 'hot' car and gave him a piece of my mind. If Mindy hadn't been watching, I think I might have also given him a piece of my fist. That was when he tried to explain he was only doing his job, that he was a reporter chasing a fast-breaking news story."

Fast-breaking news story! As if! Mitch scoffed silently. Ken Clark had only been after a single picture which he hoped would help him pay for that "hot" car and a lifestyle that was well beyond his reporter's salary.

"What, no excuses, no apparent good reason for your colleague's life-threatening behavior?" When she remained silent, he swung back to face her, challenging her.

"That kind of irresponsible behavior is inexcusable," she said, and saw amazement slowly replacing outrage in his expression.

"Yeah, well . . ." He shrugged, stymied by her reply.

"Dan, not all journalists are like the one who nearly ran down your niece." She met his gaze evenly. "But I can understand how that incident would destroy your belief in their integrity and sense of decency. Trust is a difficult thing to repair. Believe me, I know and understand. And I think we both need time to recover our ability to believe in people."

"Fine," he said, turning away. "Suits me a to a T. How about some coffee? Do you think any of those cookies are salvageable? And, by the way, what distracted you so badly you let them burn? Apparently you didn't hear my snowmobile, either. Weren't napping, were you?" He pulled off his jacket, hung it over the back of a chair, and headed for the coffeepot on the counter.

"I was reading," she said, beginning to pile spoons, bowls, and cookie sheets into the sink. "A book my mother brought down here to read last summer and left in the bookcase, a sci-fi adventure by D. J. Carson. Normally I don't read that kind of thing but I did find this particular one enjoyable."

She poured dishwashing soap over the stack of dishes.

"From the condition of these cookies, I'd say more like totally captivating," He felt the percolator, found it warm, and reached for a mug. "You didn't escape in time to save them from a fate worse than being abducted by aliens.

Isn't that the kind of tripe this Carson person writes about?"

"It's obvious you're completely unfamiliar with his work." Mitch turned on the hot-water tap and watched it make foam with the liquid detergent. "He ingeniously uses the genre to uncover many of the problems in today's society and show how these might be overcome in the future through not only knowledge and technology but also understanding and tolerance."

"Sounds interesting," he said, pouring coffee. "I'll have to read one of his epics some day when I have nothing better to do. By the way, why this sudden interest in D. J. whatever? This place is full of books. Why did you decide to read one of his today?"

Mitch paused for a moment, then turned off the tap and sat down to let the dishes soak.

"Someone I used to work with in Toronto dropped by this morning," she began, seeing no reason not to tell him an edited version of Ken's visit.

"Ah-ha!" Dan broke in, coldly triumphant. "The boyfriend from Toronto, the refresher course in bad relationships. I might have guessed! Trying to rekindle the fire, was he? He must really have it bad to chase you all the way down here." He went to the refrigerator, opened it, and peered inside.

Mitch was exasperated. "Hardly. Apparently this D. J. Carson has gone missing and there's a big reward for finding him, so naturally Ken Clark is hot on his trail. It just happened to lead here."

"The guy must be mentally deficient!" Dan swung to face her, a milk carton in his hand. "What would make a reporter think a writer like this D. J. Carson would be down here? In February?"

"Apparently Constable Stuart is his best friend." Mitch shrugged. "Ken thought D. J. might be hiding out with the mountie."

"Really? Your old flame must be quite a detective." Dan closed the refrigerator door and went to sit at the table. "And did he meet with success?"

"No," Mitch replied, brushing a few crumbs across the table. "He questioned Bradley Stuart and the good constable told him D. J. Carson definitely isn't staying with him."

"And how did he make out with you?" Dan took a sip of coffee and Mitch saw that he was watching her closely over the rim of his cup.

"No better than with his real mission," she said with a careless flip of her head. "Actually he did me an unintentional favor. He reminded me of why I'm not ready for another serious relationship, not now, maybe never."

"Had something . . . or someone made you almost forget?" He looked at her so intensely Mitch was forced to turn away, afraid of what he might see in her eyes.

"No," she lied. "But the pain had started to lessen. I needed another jab of the knife to remind me why I'm here."

"So then, he's safely on his way back home, both of his quests in vain?" Dan failed to sound indifferent and Mitch felt a little reviving ping of happiness in her heart.

"I suppose," she said with another shrug. "He tried to convince me to question some of the local people but I refused. With no other avenues to explore and no one else's help to solicit, Ken Clark isn't likely to waste any more time around here."

"Good. And like I said, some day when I have nothing better to do, I'll read something this D. J. Carson wrote." Dan looked up at her, a twinkle in his eyes, and her heart smiled back. "Then I'll be able to decide if he's worth a trip from Toronto or, more important, a batch of cookies."

"Really!" Mitch arose and went to call Sadie back inside.

"And some good has come out of today. Aside from this cookie-making being really gratifying for me, it's also distracted you from your Don Quixote quest for the poor, harried hermit," he said, munching on one of the bits of charcoal that had fallen on the oven door. He leaned back contentedly on his chair and patted Sadie who had dashed into the kitchen to sit, tail wagging eagerly, beside him. "Even burned, these things are pretty good. What are they called?

"Hermits." Mitch waved the kitchen door to and fro to clear the last of the smoke from the room.

"Hermits?" Dan stared at her, astonished. "Ah, man, you've got to be kidding! You made cookies called hermits after what you'd just been through chasing a real one?"

"I *thought* they'd be evocative to you." Mitch abandoned her fanning and pulled up a chair to sit directly across the table from him. "You can arrange for him to meet with me," she said, looking deep into his eyes with searing intensity and trying not to let the lingering smoke make her blink as she locked her gaze on his face.

"Oh, yeah, right! Like I'm supposed to bring him down here for . . ." He glanced about in exasperation. "For hermits."

"Don't get nasty." Mitch's tone grew soothing, almost a purr. "But you *do* know him, and you *do* want me to leave him alone. So it just seems you're the logical person to set up a meeting."

Dan got up and went to stare out the open door into the overcast day. For a few moments he was silent. Then, running a hand agitatedly through his hair, he turned back to Mitch. "If I can convince this poor old man to come to see you, will you promise that will be the end of it? That you'll never again attempt to visit him or bother him in any way?"

"I promise!" Mitch jumped to her feet and clapped her hands in delight. "When?"

"I don't know," he said, annoyed. "Tonight, tomorrow maybe. It'll depend on him, won't it? And did anyone ever tell you you can be about as much fun as having a Jack Russell terrier clamped onto the seat of your pants?"

"Not recently," she replied, undeterred by his remark, her face glowing triumphantly. "Thanks, Dan. I could kiss you!"

"Not now." Scowling, he zipped up his jacket. "Your old boyfriend's visit and your nagging have kicked any and all romantic notions right out the door. I may as well head upriver and try to badger that pathetic old man into coming to see you."

"Now you're trying to make me feel guilty." Mitch planted her feet squarely and stood looking directly into his face, arms akimbo. "Well, it won't work. Some human contact will be good for him. And I'll make him a nice lunch."

"Oreos?" he asked, turning back in the doorway, his teasing grin showing that his sense of humor had returned.

"Get!" Mitch ordered, but feeling a chuckle of pure delight bubbling in her throat.

She'd won!

Four hours later Mitch heard the drone of the snowmobile as she was slicing the last ham-and-cheese sandwich into neat triangles.

"Dan's coming back," she said disappointedly as Sadie braced herself against the living room sill and gave a welcoming bark as she looked out at the river into the gathering gloom of winter's twilight. "I wonder what went wrong." She went to join the dog at the window. "That's Dan's snowmobile . . . and his outfit." Even in the encroaching darkness, she could be certain of those facts.

The machine turned up over the low river back in front of the cottage and stopped. The driver shut off the engine and dismounted.

"That's not Dan!" she breathed to Sadie as the driver removed the safety helmet and long gray hair and beard escaped into view.

She watched as the man fumbled in a pocket of Dan's snowmobile jacket, took out a pair of wire-rimmed glasses, and put them on. Then, slightly stooped and with a decided limp, he started toward the cabin. In the fading light, Mitch was struck by his resemblance to pictures she had seen of the huge, hairy half-man, half-ape creature that was believed by some to roam the forests of the American northwest and was known as a Sasquatch.

Suddenly Mitch was apprehensive. In spite of Dan's dire warnings, she hadn't expected anyone like this weird, bent creature. She had also thought Dan would return with the hermit but since the older man apparently had had to borrow Dan's gear, the patroller couldn't. She and Sadie would be alone with this hairy hulk. Suddenly Mitch was afraid.

When the hermit came up onto the veranda, he paused before the window and peered in at the young woman and little dog silhouetted in the lamplight. His eyes behind tinted granny glasses were inscrutable. The rest of his features were equally eclipsed by bushy gray beard and hair, the latter hanging in ragged tangles below his broad, stooped shoulders.

He's like some kind of ape man, Mitch thought, trying to quell her shaky knees and heart. *But Dan wouldn't send him here if he were actually dangerous, would he? And lend him his snowmobile and clothes as well?*

Maybe Dan didn't lend him those things, a horrible little voice muttered in the back of her mind. *Maybe this abominable hermit took them from him! Maybe Dan is lying injured or worse out at this creature's cabin. And it's all your fault, Michelle Wallace!*

The man on the veranda, apparently satisfied with his initial perusal of the situation inside, shrugged, turned, went back down the steps, and proceeded around to the back door. A moment later he was pounding on it with a raised fist.

Get a grip and stop your crazy imaginings, Mitch, she ordered herself sternly. *This is what you've been begging for, isn't it?*

She opened the door, mustered a smile, extended her hand . . . and realized she had no idea what his name was.

"Good evening," she said. "I'm Michelle Wallace. Won't you come in?"

The hairy creature grunted, stepped inside, and accepted her hand.

"Name's Harvey," he grated in a gravelly voice. Then he pulled his hand away and made a finger V. "Peace," he said.

"Oh, yes, right, peace." Mitch stuck up corresponding fingers and noticed the filthy condition of his hands and nails. *Geraldine's eyesight must be going,* she thought. *Nothing about this guy suggests well-groomed rich man. And Dan certainly wasn't exaggerating the smelly, dirty part.* Mitch found herself fighting an urge to hold her nose.

"Dan said ya had food," he said, looking out into the brightly lit kitchen where soup bowls and sandwiches were on the table. "Said if I'd answer a few questions, ya'd feed me. Lent me his stuff to come down here, too. Nice fella, that Danny."

"Yes, he certainly is." Mitch got control of herself. "Please come in and make yourself comfortable, Mr . . ."

"Harvey, just Harvey," he muttered, following her. "But put out that big light first. Bothers my eyes."

"Oh, sure, of course." Mitch snapped off the

overhead bulb and left the cabin bathed in lamplight. "Sit here, please, and I'll get the soup."

By this time Sadie had circled the newcomer several times, sniffing. Then, slowly, her tail began to wag. Mitch felt slightly reassured.

As Harvey pulled off Dan's jacket and sat down she saw he was wearing a badly stained plaid shirt. Trying not to inhale too deeply or get any closer than was absolutely necessary, she ladled soup into his bowl.

"Smells good," he said, sitting down. He picked up the white cloth napkin she had set by his place and stuffed a corner into the top of his shirt. Then, ignoring the spoon, he took the bowl up in both hands, raised it to his lips, and slurped its contents down in a heartbeat. When he'd finished, he wiped his mouth with the back of his hand and reached for a sandwich. He consumed it in a single bite.

"Got any beer?" he asked, his words muffled by food.

"Will coffee do?" she asked as a second sandwich followed the first.

"It'll have to if you got no beer," he mumbled, spewing crumbs as he talked. "What ya want to know, anyway?"

"I wanted to know about your life." Mitch

poured coffee into a mug and shoved it quickly across the table to him, again struggling not to inhale. "I'm a writer. I'm planning a novel. I thought you might have an interesting story to tell."

Harvey paused thoughtfully for a moment, then grabbed another sandwich and stuffed it into his mouth.

"No," he said, sending out another spray of crumbs. "Been on the road since '68. My uncle died last summer. He left me that cabin upriver and a bit of money. Figured it would be a good place to hole up for the winter. Might even stay next summer if the bugs aren't too bad."

"Being a man of the road, then, I guess you definitely aren't D. J. Carson," Mitch said disappointedly. Harvey No-Last-Name was turning out to be nothing but a smelly, obnoxious tramp.

"D. J. who?"

"The writer. When a reporter friend of mine turned up here looking for him, the thought occurred to me that you might be him. . . ." Her voice trailed off.

Harvey had stopped eating and was staring at her intently.

"Ya thought I was this D. J. whatever person?"

"Well, yes, but now I realize you can't possibly be him. You don't look in the least like the man he described."

"But ya didn't know that then, right?" The eyes behind the granny glasses narrowed, becoming shockingly shrewd in a man who moments before had seemed merely a crude, bumbling lout. "Did ya tell him what ya suspected?"

"No." She shook her head, backing away from him with the coffeepot clutched in her hand and some vague idea of throwing it at him if he made a wrong move.

"So he left no better than he come?" His ability to keep focused on his questioning amazed Mitch. Moments before he'd seemed almost witless, a burnout from years of substance abuse.

"Actually worse," she said, replacing the coffeepot on its holder with a shaky hand. "He had hopes of finding D. J. Carson when he came. When he left, he had none."

"Good. 'Cause if him or anyone else starts botherin' me, I'll have to put a stop to it, ya understand?"

He arose and loomed over her, a massive shadowy presence in the small, lamplit cottage.

"Yes, of course." Mitch struggled to make

herself sound reassuring, fighting the urge to step away from him. She couldn't let him see she was afraid.

"I gotta go," he muttered. "Good grub. But remember what I said."

In less than three minutes he was roaring away into the night on Dan's snowmobile.

Mitch watched the taillight vanish into the darkness, then rushed to the telephone and began dialing the local detachment of the RCMP.

"I think we've just learned what became of D. J. Carson, Sadie," she breathed as she waited for an answer. "That creature is either holding him prisoner, or my novel is well on the way to becoming a murder mystery!"

Chapter Seven

"So what's all this about my life being in danger and poor old Harvey being some kind of homicidal maniac?" Grinning broadly, Dan stepped into the cottage out of the gray, windy morning. "Brad said you called him last night with some story about D. J. Carson being missing and how Harv knew something about it and if I wasn't already, I probably soon would be another of his victims."

Mitch, in a gray sweatsuit and Nikes, slammed the door and glared up at him, hair tangled, eyes puffy from lack of sleep.

"Thanks for caring about me, Dan," she mocked. "I'm really touched that you were concerned."

"Ah, hey, look, I am." Dan threw off his jacket and put his hands on her shoulders but she shrugged them off and swung angrily away from him. "Didn't Brad reassure you I was okay? That Harv wouldn't hurt a flea?"

"Probably that's why he looks as if he's infested with them!" Arms crossed on her chest, Mitch stared out the front window at the frozen river. "I wouldn't have had to contact Constable Stuart if I'd known how to reach you personally."

"Yeah, well, the only way to contact me up at my cabin is by shortwave radio and since I haven't seen one here, your best bet is through Brad. But feel free to do it anyway," he finished with a grin.

"Don't hold your breath, buddy."

"Okay, okay." Dan threw up his hands in surrender. "I concede. I'm a thoughtless lout. But at least let me try to make amends by helping you pack."

"Pack? I'm not going anywhere." She turned to him, surprised.

"Oh, yes, you are," he replied, scooping Sadie up into his arms to hug her. "This storm that's closing in has left a trail of destruction miles wide in its wake. Heavy snowfalls followed by freezing rain and high winds have downed power and phone lines and made roads and highways virtually impassable. It could be the storm of the century. So pack what you need. You and Sadie are heading for town."

He replaced the happy little dog on the floor.

"No way!" Mitch was excited. "This is going to make great background for my story I decided to write last night after Harvey left. You'll be my hero, a laid-back but incredibly caring camp patrol person, tough and brave and strong and gentle—"

"Will you listen to me?" Dan said angrily. "This is a murderous storm! And this summer place hasn't got a generator or wood stove or a CB radio or even a gas range for use under emergency conditions. So get packing and away from here before it's too late. And forget that story idea! The last thing I want is a book written about me."

"Will you come with me?" Before his genuine concern, Mitch quieted and spoke softly.

"No." He released her and turned away from the gentleness in her tone and expression. "There'll be lots of work for me. Brad will be short on manpower and there'll be people needing help. Right now, I have to make one more swing upriver to make sure everyone including Harvey is either out of the area or secure. And I want to know you and Sadie are safe before I go. Don't worry about your water system. I'll drain it on my way downriver."

"Dan." Mitch's voice stopped him at the door and she went to stand close behind him. "Please be careful." Her tone was soft and sincere.

Slowly he turned back to her and she stepped closer, put her arms about his neck, and kissed him lightly on the lips. Then quickly, almost shyly, she stepped back and clasped her hands behind her.

"Take care," she said, looking down at her sneakers and drawing a pattern on the floor with the toe of one.

"Yeah, sure." He paused a moment, then turned quickly and went out.

"I know, I know!" she answered Sadie's wide-eyed stare as she heard the snowmobile engine rev. "A plumber on a snowmobile! But, darn it, Sadie, I do like him . . . and I do care . . . and we're not budging an inch until he gets back here safe and sound."

Snow began at dusk—great, soft, silent flakes that at first quieted and soothed but then grew wild and aggressive, buffeting the little cottage huddled beneath the pines. Mitch, watching the storm intensify from the living room window, hugged Sadie in her arms, and smiled. She loved the uninhibited grandeur of snowstorms in the country. She wouldn't miss out on a night like this for anything.

Only one fact flawed her enjoyment of the night. Dan was somewhere out there patrolling, checking to make sure everyone in the vicinity was safe and prepared for the blizzard.

"He's strong and resourceful," she tried to reassure herself by explaining to Sadie. "He'll be just fine, don't you worry."

When Mitch awoke the next morning the blustery snowfall of the previous evening had turned to an outright blizzard laced with ice pellets. It sounded as if a giant hand was pelting each window with pebbles. Gale-force winds ripped through the branches of the pines and made them roar and moan. The cottage seemed locked in the powerful grip of some huge and monstrous force.

Mitch hugged Sadie to her and snuggled down in her quilts.

"As soon as Dan comes back, we'll leave," she promised the little dog.

Five minutes later she got up, pulled on her robe and slippers, and headed for the kitchen.

As she passed the thermostat she shivered and paused to turn up the heat.

"Must be the intensity of the storm," she told Sadie. "That setting is usually high enough to keep this place warm. Oh, well, we'll be comfortable again in a few minutes. I'll get the coffee going before I shower. Then we'll have breakfast and wait for Dan."

In spite of the storm, Mitch felt safe and even happy. These feelings, she admitted as she ran water into the percolator, were because of Dan Jeffrey and his eminent return.

"What am I doing, Sadie?" she asked as she measured out coffee. "I'm falling for that guy and both he and the timing are all wrong. I've got to put a stop to it right now."

She flicked the switch on the coffeepot and turned toward the bathroom with a shiver.

"It's awfully chilly in here. Why is it taking so long to warm up?" She bent and put a hand on a baseboard heater. It was stone cold. Apprehensively she straightened and flicked on a light switch. Nothing.

"Oh, no!" she moaned. "The power lines must be down!"

She hurried to the window and looked out at her Jeep. All that was visible was a six-inch-wide strip of roof and the radio antenna. The drive behind it was choked with six-foot snow-drifts.

"We're trapped, Sadie!" she breathed. "There's no way out! And we've no power, heat, or"—she paused and put the telephone receiver to her ear—"phone."

She sank dejectedly into a chair in the living room, pulled her robe more closely about her, and shivered. "I'm cold," she said, hugging Sadie who had climbed up beside her. "Cold, and I need a cup of coffee and a hot shower. Why don't I ever listen to Dan?"

Then her gaze fell on the fireplace and the woodbin filled with logs and kindling beside it.

"Dan opened up the chimney!" she cried, jumping to her feet. "We'll make a fire, Sadie, and I'll hang Mom's old tin teapot on its spit to heat water for coffee."

Within a few minutes, she had a fire blazing cheerfully in the old stone hearth and stood back to admire her handiwork.

"I'm glad Dad taught me how to do that," she said. "Now" she rubbed her hands together in anticipation—"coffee."

She returned to the kitchen and rummaged through cupboards under the sink until she found her mother's battered metal teapot. The family had used it on picnics to boil water over open fires.

"Ah-ha!" she cried triumphantly, holding it aloft for Sadie to see. "Now all we need is water!"

She turned on the tap and waited. A thin stream of water trickled slowly into the pot, then receded to large, limp drips before stopping entirely.

"What . . . Oh, no! Of course! The electric pump won't work either. I just put the last of our water in the percolator. Sadie, we're in deep, deep trouble!"

She placed the teapot on the counter and shoved her tangled hair back with nervous fingers. While the idea of being trapped in a wilderness cabin in a blizzard might be exciting, even romantic, if you were with your significant other and rescue was not totally out of the question and your basic creature comforts were still available, this reality definitely wasn't. She wished her father hadn't seen fit to replace their old gas range with that shiny new electric one that past summer.

Panicking wasn't an option. Mitch drew a deep breath and forced herself to think calmly and logically. She had some fuel and food and orange juice and soft drinks and milk. She and

Sadie could survive for a couple of days. By that time, Dan would return. In that fact she felt completely confident.

Taking care not to spill a single, precious drop, she transferred the water from percolator to teapot, kept enough aside to brush her teeth, and headed back to the fireplace to heat it.

As the morning wore on, the storm intensified. Precipitation turned to freezing rain, hardening the colossal snowdrifts in place and weighting down the trees about the cabin until they bent and creaked and groaned beneath the torturous pressure.

When Mitch tried the doors to let Sadie out, she found them frozen shut. After much shoving and hacking with a long butcher knife she finally managed to push the kitchen door open a slit wide enough to allow the little dog to get out.

"Come right back, babe," she said as Sadie squirmed through the slot. "It's a horrible day."

She had tied a length of rope to the dog's collar to ensure she did. She didn't want the loyal, clever little creature attempting to go for help as she had that night upriver.

The blast of icy air and sleet that hit Mitch as she stood waiting for Sadie told her Dan had probably been right. This could well be the storm of the century. *Oh, well*, she thought, struggling to retain her optimism as she drew Sadie back inside. *We're going to be okay. We have fuel and food. And Dan will be back soon. I'll just have to bury myself in a good book until he arrives.*

The day, however, soon seemed interminable. With windows half covered with crusted snowdrifts, the cottage was darkened and Mitch found she had to light one of the oil lamps in order to read. The wind kept up a constant roar through the trees, rattled shutters, and hurled hard bits of frozen precipitation against the windows. At times Mitch felt the little cottage tremble beneath its onslaught. This time she discovered even the magic of D. J. Carson's writing couldn't distract her from her circumstances. With an exasperated sigh, she finally tossed the book aside and stared at the woodbin next to the fireplace with growing alarm.

The neat stack of logs her father had left for emergencies at the end of the summer and which had seemed so comfortingly large early in the day had diminished by evening to a unnerving few.

"We'll just have to conserve," she told Sadie more confidently than she felt. "We'll wrap ourselves in quilts for the night so we won't need too much fire to keep warm."

But as darkness fell and the cottage grew shadowy and cold, Mitch loosened her resolve and put two of the largest of the few remaining precious logs on the fire. As she returned to her place with Sadie among a tangle of quilts and pillows on the couch, visions of Harvey, weird and apelike like peering in at her out of the storm rose up to haunt her.

"He's just a simple, harmless old man," she tried to reassure herself by talking aloud, but at that moment the wind rose to new screaming heights, a shutter blown loose in the gale banged, and she cried out in fear, burying her face in Sadie's neck.

"I-I'm scared, Sadie." She shuddered. "Mitch Wallace, tough city reporter, is scared. Dan, where are you? Why don't you come?"

A sick feeling was welling up inside her. Dan would never willingly desert her, she knew. If he didn't come, it was because something terrible had happened to him. What if he'd been wrong about Harvey's being harmless? What if Harvey had seen Dan's concerned visit as the intrusion the hermit had warned her about? What if he'd done something heinous to Dan? She couldn't bear to think of that possibility. A future without Dan Jeffrey would be black and cold and pointless.

"Come back to me, Danny, please come back," she begged aloud, rocking Sadie in her arms.

In spite of her terror, Mitch was finally overcome by exhaustion and she dozed. Suddenly she was shocked to wakefulness by a huge crash. Something had broken into the kitchen. With trembling hands she took up the lamp and cautiously made her way through the archway.

To her utter dismay she saw several feet of a massive pine protruding through the window above her computer. Her monitor, thrown from the desk by the impact, lay smashed on the floor. Arctic-cold wind was whistling in through the damage.

"No! Oh, no!" Mitch despaired. "Now we'll never stay warm! We're going to die, Sadie!"

Chapter Eight

Mitch was miserably cold. She had tried to block the gaping hole in the kitchen window as best she could with quilts and blankets but still slender, icy fingers of the storm managed to hiss through cracks in her barricade of bedclothes. The temperature inside the cottage was rapidly dropping toward equaling that of the outdoors.

Her supply of firewood had diminished to a pair of logs already crumpling to ash in the fireplace. The oil in her lamps almost bottomed out, continued to sink at an insidiously continuous pace. In a further effort to stay warm she had donned her snowsuit, boots, cap, and mitts. Then, convinced she had done all she could in her efforts to survive, she huddled in a corner of the couch with Sadie in her arms.

"Look what I've done to you again, babe," she said to the little dog. "You are such an intelligent little girl. It's a tragedy your caregiver is a total disaster. You deserve so much better."

Sadie only snuggled closer.

"Don't," Mitch whispered, dangerously close to tears. "Don't be kind. I don't deserve it."

Then Sadie stiffened alertly and pricked her ears.

"What? Babe, did you hear something?"

The next moment there was a pounding at her front door.

"Mitch, Mitch, are you in there? Answer me!"

"Dan!" Mitch scrambled to her feet and stumbled to the door. "Dan, we're here! But I can't get the door open!"

"Pull!" he yelled. "Pull!"

And she did as he crashed against it from outside with his shoulder.

The frozen panel gave and the man burst into the room, almost tumbling over Mitch and Sadie, who was close behind her.

"Dan! Oh, Dan! We . . . I was so scared! We

should have left like you said. "I'll never ignore your advice again! Never!" She stood in the center of the room, hands clenched into white-knuckled fists at her sides, babbling.

"Stop! Stop it, Mitch!" he ordered, clutching her against his snow-encrusted jacket.

He was holding her so tightly she felt as if the breath was being crushed out of her body, but she didn't care. In her dazed state she could only think that Dan was with her and she was safe, safe at last.

Then he pulled her out from him and in the shadowy glow of guttering oil lamps, looked down into her face.

"You used the front door," she said inanely. "You never use the front door."

"Because the kitchen one is blocked by that tree," he said. "Now, come on. Snap out of it. We have to get out of here right away. Put on your warmest clothes and get your toothbrush. You won't be coming back here for a while but we don't have room for anything else. I'll wrap Sadie in a jacket to keep her warm. She'll have to ride in front of me on the snowmobile. While you're getting ready, I'll turn on the outside taps and drain your pipes so they won't freeze. Move! There's no time to waste!"

She could only nod and obey.

Ten minutes later they were speeding up-river through the inky blackness of the storm-tortured night on Dan's snowmobile. Mitch, her face covered in a scarf, her jacket hood tied tightly under her chin, clung to Dan, her arms around his waist, her cheek pressed against his broad back. She wondered how he managed to drive through that terrible night with only the bobbing beam of his headlight to guide him and with Sadie wrapped in one of her father's jackets held in front of him. Then she gave up trying to understand and allowed herself to re-lax into the sheer trust and relief that she and Sadie were in his care.

It was too dark and Mitch was too nearly frozen when they got to Dan's cabin to notice anything about the outside. But once he had helped her and Sadie struggle through the drifts and storm to its dark interior she was imme-diately suffused with its wonderful warmth.

Immensely relieved, she huddled just inside the door and waited while Dan turned on a light suspended in the center of the raw-beamed ceiling.

The room that emerged out of the darkness was an astonishing one. Log walls chinked with what looked like clay surrounded an area that had two distinctly different furniture types.

Near the door a rectangular, airtight wood stove gave off a reviving warmth. A maple rocking chair, the finish worn from its arms, faced the stove, a threadbare green hassock in front of it, an overflowing magazine rack by its side. Beside the stove, reaching from the scarred plank floor to the ceiling, was a pile of firewood. Along the wall to her right was a cracked and sagging brown leather couch.

The back of the room was a sharp antithesis to the front. Modern oak cupboards with a gleaming stainless steel sink and a sparkling gas range, refrigerator, and freezer made it look highly convenient but completely out of character in their setting. The only concession in that area to the cabin's pioneer ambience was a rough plank table with equally crude benches on either side.

The other pieces of furniture in the room were a huge rolltop mahogany desk covered with loose papers with a CB radio perched on one corner, a captain's chair shoved in at it, and a floor-to-ceiling bookcase constructed of boards and bricks that stretched from the desk to the cabin's front wall along the left side of the room next to one of the cabin's small windows. Crammed with books, those rudimentary shelves could provide several months' entertainment for most avid readers. She was surprised. After Dan's remarks about reading D. J. Carson only when he had nothing better to do, she'd decided he wasn't of a literary bent. Still, he could quote Robert Frost. . . .

"Make yourself at home." Dan interrupted her perusal of the cabin by turning to her with a wide, welcoming smile. Then, suddenly, as if struck by a thought, he strode to the desk, shoved the papers into a top drawer, turned its key, and dropped it into his pocket.

"Let me have your jacket," he continued, pulling his off. "I'll hang it up by the stove to dry."

"Thanks," she said, removing her mittens, hood, and jacket and handing them to him. "May Sadie have some water?" She knelt and freed the little dog from the sleet-encrusted jacket she had been wearing for the drive. "I didn't have very much to give her today."

"Sure." Dan finished hanging their clothing by the stove and went to the cupboard to get a bowl. "If you'd like to warm up faster, you can take a hot shower." He indicated one of two doorways to the left of the room. "There's a robe on a hook behind the door. Just throw your clothes out and I'll dry them by the fire."

"That sounds like a small piece of heaven,"

she said. "But how do you manage all this—hot water, etc.?"

"I have an oil-powered generator and several tanks of propane." Dan turned on a tap, filled the bowl, and squatted to place it before the thirsty little dog. "We can't afford to be wasteful, mind you, but you are chilled to the bone."

Mitch started for the bathroom but paused in its doorway and looked back at him.

"Thanks," she said softly. "Thanks for once again saving my heedless hide."

The bathroom she discovered was small, just large enough to contain a newly installed shower stall, toilet, and vanity. Pushed to the back under a single small window was a stand holding a basin and ewer.

She grinned. That small washstand had probably been the cabin's entire answer to a facility until Dan the plumber-by-trade had moved in. Humming as she removed her clothes, she glanced over the small array of male toiletries on the vanity. She was surprised to see Dan's brand of aftershave was one of the most expensive. She knew because during a shopping expedition with Ken Clark, her former colleague had expressed his desire for the product.

"That would make nice gift for the man in

your life," he'd suggested bluntly. "If my credit card wasn't maxed out, I'd buy it myself."

Mitch had picked up the bottle, ready to grant him his wish. Then she'd seen the price.

"Look at that!" she'd cried. "You'd have to be a millionaire to even consider it!"

"Well, your old man is or nearly is," Ken had persisted. "So what's the big deal?"

"The fact that Dad has money doesn't mean I do," she'd replied, feeling a rare moment of genuine annoyance with Ken as she'd replaced the container on the counter. "And please call him Joe or Mr. Wallace, not 'the old man.' "

How can an unemployed plumber afford something like that? she wondered, turning the bottle over in her hand to make certain it was the correct brand and not a generic look alike.

Convinced that it was the authentic item, she replaced it carefully on the vanity and took the thick navy robe from its hook on the back of the door. Its label identified it as a purchase from one of Toronto's most exclusive men's clothing boutiques. Once again, courtesy of Ken Clark, she knew.

Puzzled, she replaced the robe on its hook and turned on the shower. Were the robe and aftershave "treat" items Dan had purchased when he'd taken his niece on holiday to Canada's Wonderland or was he hiding some deep, dark secret about his life and finances? As she stepped out of the shower, she shivered in spite of the warmth of the water. Being trapped in an isolated cabin with a man whose past grew more mysterious by the minute was not a soul-warming condition.

Twenty minutes later, swathed from head to heels in Dan's elegant robe, wet hair brushed back from her face, she emerged to find him placing two steaming bowls of chili on the table. A plate of bread and cheese was in the center with two thick candles on either side. He had turned off the light and now only the candles and an old-fashioned oil lamp on the desk by the window illuminated the cabin's interior. The room was cozy and warm and safe and dangerously romantic, Mitch thought as she listened to the storm howling beyond its sturdy walls and looked at the incredibly handsome man in plaid flannel shirt and jeans fixing her supper.

Dan looked up at her and smiled.

"Feeling better?" he asked, replacing the cooking pot on the stove.

"Yes, much." She hesitated uncertainly.

"Dan, you really don't have to treat me like a guest. I . . . I don't deserve it."

"No, you don't," he said. "You've been willful and heedless and downright reckless. But I still happen to like you a lot. Come. Sit."

A rueful little smile curled her lips and she padded forward on her bare feet to join him as he indicated a bench at the table.

"You need socks," he said, and went into the other room Mitch assumed was his bedroom. He came back with a pair of gray woolen ones. "Let me put them on for you." He knelt before her.

He knelt and began to pull a large gray woolen sock over her left foot.

"Now I know how that guy in Cinderella must have felt when he saw the perfect little foot of his perfect little lady fit into her perfect little shoe." He grinned, looking up at her as he held her sock-ensconced foot.

"I'd say that's a far cry from a glass slipper," she said, cocking her head to one side to look down at the oversized sock. "But it also feels a lot cozier on a night like this. Please proceed, Prince Charming."

"Your servant, ma'am." He bowed again to his task.

When he had finished, he remained on one

knee before her, cradling her woolen-covered foot in his hands.

"You know, at any time, you're a very beautiful woman," he said softly, looking up at her. "But at this moment, in candlelight, you're completely bewitching. If I allowed myself to follow my instincts . . . but"—he released her foot and got abruptly to his feet, his tone changing with the move—"I won't. You're not ready for another relationship and I'm not in a position to offer one."

He turned, went to the wood stove, and put another log into it. Mitch was left with a wildly beating heart, her whole being awash with emotions, her pulse racing. What was she going to do with Dan Jeffrey, about him? She knew a moment of decision was fast approaching.

"I couldn't help noticing you have excellent taste," she said, fingering the rich collar of the robe. "This robe and your aftershave . . ."

"Hardly seem the likely purchases of a mostly unemployed plumber," he finished, shutting the door of the stove with a sharp click. "You're right." He turned back to face her. "Both were Christmas gifts from my sister-in-law. She took Mindy to the Santa Claus Parade in Toronto in November and did her Christmas shopping at the same time. I know she meant well, but a robe like that and an outrageously priced bottle of 'come-and-get-me' were hardly practical given my present circumstances." He shook his head, chuckling as he headed back to the kitchen area.

"So you're not a Toronto millionaire incognito?" She planted her elbows on the table, cupped her chin in her hands, and watched him closely.

"Sorry. I'm just a guy who likes looking out for beautiful women and their dogs."

"Sadie certainly seems well satisfied with your service," she said, swinging around to look at the little red dog asleep on the couch.

"While you were in the shower, she had a bowl of leftover meatloaf and went right to bed," Dan said, going over to pat the exhausted little animal. "She's a great little lady."

"Yes, she is," Mitch said softly. "I shudder to think what might have happened to me if it hadn't been for her . . . and you this past week."

"I'm sure you're completely self-reliant in the city," he said. "Here, in winter, you're faced with an entirely unfamiliar situation. Remember the fable of the city mouse and the country mouse?"

"Now you're either being kind or condescending," she said, and took a spoonful of chili. "Mmmm. This is great. You really can cook. I feel the urge to propose to you . . . again."

"And mean it?" Dan paused and looked over at her, his blue eyes becoming serious in the flickering light.

"No," she said abruptly, and returned her attention to her food. "You've just saved Sadie and me—again—and we're trapped in a wilderness cabin locked in the jaws of a blizzard with candlelight doing a number on our senses. No, it's definitely not the moment for a serious, rational proposal. By the way, what happened to your electric light?"

She gestured toward the ceiling in an attempt to change the subject.

"Man, you have to be the master of the non-sequitur!" he breathed. "Well, since you obviously want to change the subject, I turned off the light because we have to conserve generator fuel and propane. It wasn't intended to be a romantic move."

He reached for a piece of cheese and bit sharply into it.

"I know that," she said gently. "Like Brad

Stuart said, you're not a man who takes advantage of a situation."

"Oh, so you know all about me, do you?" He got to his feet so abruptly that his bench legs screeched over the rough planks of the floor, startling Sadie awake. "Then I suppose you know I have this wild attraction to you, one I have to keep mentally slapping myself to contain. And yet that I really want nothing to do with you because of your profession. And that in spite of the fact, you never cease to intrigue me, to irritate me, and to give me this feeling that I want to take care of you for the rest of my life. I'm even afraid I might be falling in—"

"Dan, no." Mitch caught his hand. "Don't say any more. There are things about me you don't know . . . things that could change all those wonderful things you think you feel for me."

"I know you're a reporter, a member of the paparazzi who I can only regard as an anathema, and, to my astonishment, I've discovered it doesn't matter. So unless you're about to tell me you are an ax murderer, don't expect to turn me off."

"Try burglar," she replied softly without taking her gaze from his face.

"What?" The incredulity in his tone equaled the surprise on his face. "Come off it, Mitch. That's not very funny. I deserve better than a bad joke."

"It wasn't meant to be funny." She released his hand, clasped hers on the table in front of her, and stared at their clenched fingers. "I was arrested breaking into a city councilor's office in Toronto last month."

"Why would you do something like that?" Incredulously he turned to her in the shadowy candlelight. "What would make an intelligent woman like you do such a crazy thing?"

"Because I was a fool," she said, lowering her head and shaking it slowly. "And because I became involved with someone I shouldn't have."

"Tell me," he said, returning to the chair opposite her. He covered her tightly clasped hands with warm, protective ones and looked deep into her troubled eyes. "Tell me." The last was so full of honest caring she couldn't refuse.

When she had finished speaking, Dan was still holding her hands.

"I'd like to get my hands on that miserable . . ." he muttered.

"It's over," she said softly. "And throttling

Ken Clark, attractive as that sounds, won't change things. I only wish my parents hadn't been dragged into it."

"Do you know what I wish?" he said, his eyes full of a tenderness that made her heart ache.

"What?" she said, her voice barely above a whisper.

"That this guy—this Clark Kent—"

"Ken Clark." She couldn't suppress the little smile that bubbled to the surface at his mistake.

"Whatever. I wish he hadn't shattered your faith in people, in men in particular. I know how fragile trust is and once it's broken, how it can often take a small miracle to restore it."

"Dan . . ." She reached out and touched his clean-shaven jaw with her fingertips, too overcome by his understanding to continue.

"Don't." He caught her hand and pulled it down, palm open, to press it to his lips.

Her throat airlocked. The man was actually taking her breath away! And all with a simple kiss on the hand.

"Danny, I—" she began when he finally raised his head and she found she could exhale.

"Don't say it, Mitch. Not now. Not while we're alone here like this. Not while we're still burying our ghosts," he said softly. "I'm not made of steel. I can only handle so much and I don't want to make any mistakes. Definitely not any that might hurt you."

He arose slowly. "Now I think it's time we went to bed. Your honesty has brought me to the verge of a confession of my own and, given what you've just told me, I don't think you'd take my story very well just now."

"Try me," she breathed softly. "In spite of my frequent bouts of recklessness and reper- toire of caustic remarks, I can be pretty darn compassionate and understanding."

"I know you can," he said, looking down at her in the candlelight. "I know you're caring and loving and a little bit of everything else that I admire. That's why I can't afford to rush into a confession that could end any chance we have at a future together. I have to sleep on it, decide what's the best way to tell you all about me."

"Dan, I've just told you I committed a se- rious crime under the influence of what I thought was love. You were able to handle it. Give me the same chance to accept whatever it is you have to say."

"No," he said softly, determinedly, and ran his knuckles slowly down her cheek. "I won't risk blowing anything that can be this great with a few ill-chosen words. Words, you see, my sweetheart, are the most powerful critters in the world."

"Dan." Her breath was hurting her, her heart cracking.

"Come on," he said, moving away, his tone reverting to normal. "We need rest and time to think. You can use my bed. I changed the sheets while you were in the shower. I'll sleep out here where I can keep an eye on the stove. Can't risk letting it go out on a night like this."

"That's just a modest way of being gallant." Mitch saw he wouldn't change his resolve and adopted his manner. "But I am grateful."

"I'm trying," he replied. "But it's not easy. You look entirely too appealing in that robe and those socks."

"Hmmm." Mitch looked down at her attire. "It must be a fetish. I doubt there's any other man on the planet who'd find me alluring in this getup."

"Could be they're the ones with the problem," he said as he lit an oil lamp to lead her into the bedroom. "If they can't recognize something really good when they see it."

Thinking she would find a crude bunk, Mitch was amazed to see a wide double bed complete with snow-white sheets, pillows, and a plump black-and-white duvet.

In contrast, an old scarred dresser with a crazed mirror, a ewer, and basin on its top sat beside a window at the rear of the room. The two outer walls were chinked logs while those used as room dividers were of rough-hewn plank like the door. Several of Dan's shirts were on hangers on nails driven into one of them.

"You'll enjoy the bed," he said. "It's a five-star hotel model. Like the kitchen appliances, I brought it with me when I moved in. I believe in roughing it in comfort."

"A man after my own heart," Mitch said, testing the mattress with her hand. "Yes, Dan Jeffrey, you're definitely of the same mind as I am on that subject. I could get pretty darn comfortable here."

"Really?" He placed the lamp on the dresser beside the basin and turned to her. "Then tomorrow we seriously have to work on exorcising those ghosts that stand in our way."

In the soft half light he personified the cliché of tall, dark, and handsome topped off with a healthy helping of strength and virility. Acutely aware of the disturbing stirrings becoming stronger by the second within her, Mitch forced herself to turn away.

"I'm really tired." She faked a yawn. "Must be all the fresh air."

"Yeah, me too. We'd better hit the sack." Dan started to pass her to leave the room, then paused beside her.

He leaned toward her, cupped her chin in his hand, and touched his lips lightly to hers.

"Tomorrow," he said softly, the single word so lingering that Mitch's self-control and common sense evaporated in a single puff.

The lamplight flickered softly over his features, the wind howled about their snug retreat, and Mitch dissolved into Michelle—Michelle who loved Dan Jeffrey and wanted him with every fiber of her being.

"Tomorrow," he only repeated firmly and left the room. "Sleep well."

"You too," she said, her voice barely above a cracking whisper. The butterflies inside her were fluttering up another marathon.

Ten minutes later, cozily ensconced in his five-star bed beneath his state-of-the-art goose-down duvet, Mitch hugged Sadie in the darkness and listened to the gale howl down the chimney and around the cabin.

"Dan?" she asked softly through the door

which she had left open at his suggestion to allow the heat from the stove to enter.

"Anything wrong?" His voice came reassuringly back and she heard the springs of the old couch creak as he rolled over.

"No," she said. "I was just thinking how nice it is not to be alone tonight. Are you ever lonely way up here by yourself?"

"Sometimes." His voice was soft and soothing in the dark, storm-engulfed cabin. "But not tonight. It's nice to have you and Sadie here, Mitch. Just feels right, our being together, doesn't it?"

Chapter Nine

Mitch awoke in the comforting warmth of
Dan's bed to daylight struggling in at the window and the storm still raging around the
cabin. Sadie, curled up beside her, stretched
and yawned languidly, apparently feeling as
safe and comfortable as her mistress.

"Morning, babe." Mitch rubbed the dog's
head. "Sleep well?"

In answer Sadie leaped to the plank floor and
stood, paws braced, tail wagging, waiting for
her friend to get up.

"Okay, okay." Mitch arose with a chuckle.
Still wearing Dan's robe and socks, she padded
into the other room, finger-combing her hair as
she went.

"About time." Dan, seated at the desk, shoved the paper and pen he'd been using into a drawer and arose to greet her with a broad grin. Mitch noticed he failed to lock it this time. "It's nearly ten o'clock."

In a faded blue denim shirt and jeans, he looked like the star of a country music video, one designed to rivet every woman's eyes to the screen. The cabin, its small windows largely obscured by snow and ice, let in little of the storm-darkened morning light. Dan had lighted two oil lamps, one on his desk and the other in the center of the kitchen table. The effect was an atmosphere almost as cozy and romantic as the previous evening.

And I'm storm-stayed in a wilderness cabin with the critter, Mitch moaned inwardly. *Give me strength.*

"Really?" She turned away and stifled a phony yawn, feeling far from languid. "I must have slept like a log. You made coffee?"

"Help yourself," he said, indicating a pot on the stove, and went to add another log to the fire in the wood stove.

She did as he offered, ordering her thoughts back into the prim-and-proper area.

"You have the makings for an excellent omelet," she said as she opened the refrigerator door and perused its contents. Holding the door ajar, she turned back to him. "I could whip up a couple for us if you'd like. I seem to recall you once said I'd have to make you a full-course meal if you ever had to save my heedless hide again."

"You know how?" Dan's blue eyes were twinkling. "After the cookies . . ."

"You have an annoyingly long memory," she said, turning back to the refrigerator. "I may not bake very well but I am a pretty fine cook. I'll get dressed and prove it to you."

She started toward the bedroom, coffee cup in hand, then turned back to him. "You can finish your . . . letter, if you like. I won't disturb you."

"Letter? Oh, right." He pulled aside a threadbare curtain and looked out the front window into the snow and rain coiling around the cabin. "Well, there's really no hurry. I'm not likely to mail it today, am I?"

He flashed her a rueful grin and returned his gaze to the outdoors. But as Mitch grabbed her jeans and sweater from the hooks where they had been drying by the stove and headed into the bedroom, she couldn't help wondering why he had hidden an unimportant letter so quickly.

Had Dan been writing to a woman, a woman significant in his life?

"By the way," he said just before she closed the door. "I managed to contact Brad on the CB early this morning and asked him to let your parents know you're safe."

"Well, thank you." Mitch paused and turned back to him in amazement. "That was thoughtful. Mom and Dad will be much relieved. But how could Constable Stuart know where to find them? Toronto is a big city and Joe Wallace isn't an uncommon name."

"Brad has the names, addresses, and telephone numbers of all the cottage and camp owners in the area," he said. "That way, if I find any irregularities on my rounds, he knows where to get in contact with them immediately."

"Of course! My brain must have frozen last night and is just starting to thaw. Anyway, thanks again. I should have thought of contacting them myself—they must have been frantic when they heard about the storm and then, no daily e-mail from me—but I assumed there was no way of reassuring them until we got to a telephone or computer. I forgot about your radio. You're a good man, Dan Jeffrey. I appreciate the fact."

Then she turned and went into the bedroom, closing the door behind her.

Later in the bathroom as she washed her face and brushed her teeth, however, Mitch felt a sinking feeling in the pit of her stomach. Dan Jeffrey was a good man, a trustworthy man, an all-around terrific man.

But he had a secret he couldn't bring himself to tell her. Dan Jeffrey had been concerned with hiding something he'd been writing. A letter to a woman? she wondered, her heart plummeting, a woman whose memory made a relationship with Mitch impossible, who was the ghost he had not managed to exorcise?

We have to clear the air today, she resolved, giving her hair a final flick with his brush. *We can't go on like this.*

"You never told me very much about yourself," Mitch said twenty minutes later as they sat at the table with omelets, toast, and coffee in front of them. "For all I know you could have a dark and mysterious past and here I am, stranded in a wilderness cabin with you." She made a pretense of teasing to cover up a major fishing expedition.

"Not much to know," he surprised her by responding easily. "My dad owned a plumbing supply business in Winnipeg until he retired last year. My brother operates it now. Dad and Mom are in Bermuda for the winter."

"You only have one sibling?" she asked, his description too simple and brief to satisfy her.

"One's enough." He grinned ruefully. "Tony, Mindy's father, is a top-notch accountant and a workaholic who doesn't have the time to take his only child on vacation but has always managed to make me look like a laid-back bum. I'm sure Dad's company will reach franchise level in a couple of years under his guidance."

"But you have a trade." Mitch was surprised to hear herself defending him. "You're a plumber."

"An unemployed one," he reminded her. "Without a single business suit to my name."

"Big deal," she said and bit into her toast with a crunch.

"Now, that's amazing." He cradled his coffee cup in both hands and rocked back onto the rear legs of his chair. "A couple of days ago your eyes told me it was."

"Well . . ." Mitch felt herself growing uncomfortably warm under his perceptiveness. "I didn't really know you then."

"And you think you do now?"

His blue eyes had lost their twinkle and become intensely serious.

"Well, yes, I guess." He was making her uncomfortable. "I know you're a brave, decent man who cares about people and"—she looked over at Sadie sitting adoringly at his feet—"animals. But I'm curious about your friendship with Brad Stuart. How did you meet?"

"At college," he replied, and took a sip of coffee, watching her guardedly over the rim of his cup.

"At plumber college?" she asked, pausing in spreading strawberry jam on her second slice of toast. Her tone mirrored her astonishment.

"No, later, at the University of Manitoba." He chuckled. "Brad was studying law and I was finishing off a Master of Arts degree." He took another sip of coffee and waited for her reaction.

"You have a Master's?" She gaped at him as if he'd just told her he was an alien in disguise. "But you said you were a plumber!"

"By trade," he said, replacing his cup on the table. "Eat your toast. It's getting cold. And don't look so shocked. It's not as if I'd just told you I was a serial killer."

"But then why . . . ?"

"Did I do plumbing?" he finished. "Because

a Master's in English Lit only qualifies me to teach . . . if I added a few education courses to it. And I have no desire to be a teacher. I prefer to work with my hands, do my own thing, create my own stuff, choose my own hours."

"Ah, a free spirit, not unlike our friend Harvey." She leaned back in her chair and watched him through narrowed eyes. "No ties, no . . . significant other?"

"Not entirely unlike Harvey," he agreed. "But a tad cleaner. And definitely no significant other . . . yet."

He looked at her with such obvious meaning in his eyes, she immediately felt relieved but also embarrassed that he had so easily seen through the intent of her query. Quickly she changed the subject.

"Did you ever meet Brad Stuart's friend, the internationally famous D. J. Carson?" she asked, an astonishing suspicion beginning to rise in her mind.

"Man, there goes another of your famous nonsequiturs!" he breathed. "Did it sound as if I had when you told me reading one of *his* books caused you to burn *my* cookies?"

"No, but . . ."

"Then enough for now. I have to check the

generator." He arose and went to get his boots. "It's in the shed out back."

"You mean you're going out in that?" Mitch pointed to a window heavily laced with ice. "It's too dangerous. I can hear trees cracking and breaking in that wind every few minutes."

"I have to," he said, sitting down to pull on his boots. "The generator will be getting low on oil. I can't risk letting it run out. When I get back we'll talk. We've got to get rid of all ghosts once and for all."

He rose and put on his jacket. "Don't go outside while I'm gone, do you hear?" He slapped a fur hat on his head and picked up a pair of heavy gloves. "I mean it."

He leaned forward to plant a light kiss on her cheek.

"I promise," she said meekly.

"Now where have I heard that before?" he muttered, and went out taking Sadie with him.

Once he was gone and Mitch had watched him struggle out of sight around the corner of the cabin, she dashed to the desk and pulled open the unlocked drawer into which he had thrust the sheet of paper. She knew it was wrong, invading his privacy like that, but she had to know if what she was beginning to suspect was a fact.

The drawer was filled with a huge stack of pages, all covered with similar handwriting. Stealthily she took out a couple of the top sheets and began to read aloud:

" 'When Zee left the host planet of Albin, he hoped he'd never see it or its bloodthirsty humanoids again—' "

"Yes!" Mitch gripped the pages and yelped triumphantly. "I knew it! Dan is D. J. Carson!"

Before she could fully appreciate her find, above the moan of the wind, a sharp crackling rent the air. The next instant Sadie hit the door barking incessantly, jumping and scratching.

"What is it, girl?" Mitch threw the papers on the desk and flew to the door. When she opened it she saw the little red dog frantically dancing to the corner of the cabin and back again, barking in obvious distress.

"Dan!" In an instant she had pulled on her boots, jacket, and toque and was following Sadie around the corner of the cabin in the driving wind and freezing rain.

When she came in view of the shed at the rear of the cabin she gasped. Dan lay sprawled on his face a few feet from its door, a broken section of a big maple pinning him to the snow.

"Dan!" she cried, stumbling to him and dropping to her knees. "Oh, Danny!"

"Sounds good," he muttered, his breath coming in gasps. "Tell me you'll call me that every once in a while."

"Be quiet!" she snapped. "I've got to get this limb off of you!"

She pushed and pulled, found a strength she wouldn't have believed she possessed, and moved the massive branch just enough to allow Dan to crawl free.

"Can you get up? Can you walk?" she asked, kneeling, panting beside him in the downpour.

"Can I walk?" he scoffed and started to struggle to his knees. "Of course I can—"

He stumbled and fell flat with a grunt Mitch knew came out of pain.

"Here, let me help you," she said, water sluicing down her face.

She bent until he could get an arm about her shoulders, then stumbling under his weight, straightened up. Together they staggered to the cabin, up the steps, and all but fell through the door.

Once Mitch had deposited him on the couch, she kicked off her boots, flung aside her dripping jacket and hat, and knelt in front of him, her face grim with concern.

"Do you think I can take your jacket off without hurting you?" she asked gently.

"What kind of a wimp do you think I am?" He grimaced, starting to remove his outerwear. "I can still undress . . . myself. Ahhh—!"

"Sure you can." Mitch's tone was condescending as she moved quickly to help him.

Once he was out of his jacket, he began to fumble with the buttons of his denim shirt.

"My shoulders feel wet," he said, and Mitch saw his fingers were trembling. "And my left arm won't move."

"Here, let me." She brushed aside his hands and finished unbuttoning it for him.

"Why, Miss Michelle, ma'am," he struggled to joke. "Do you think this quite proper?"

"Quite necessary," she said as she arose and started to ease the shirt away from him. His grunt of pain stopped her just as she saw the wide wet stripe of blood across his shoulders.

"Danny, you've been cut," she said, struggling to sound calm. "We'll have to get this shirt off so that I can put some salve and a bandage on the wound."

"Okay," he said, easing his shoulders away from the back of the couch with a grimace. "Go for it."

Fighting the nausea she felt rising in her

stomach, Mitch gently peeled the bloodsoaked denim from his back and down his arms. The red slash that reached completely across Dan's broad shoulders made her flinch.

"How does it look, doc?" he asked as she knelt to unbutton the cuffs.

"Not too bad," she lied, finishing at his wrists and easing the shirt away from him.

"Well, it smarts like the blazes," he muttered. "Do you mind putting a little of the ointment from my first aid kit on it? I could stand a couple of the painkillers, too. You'll find them in the bathroom cabinet."

"It needs to be cleaned first," she said, and started to get up. "I'll get a basin and some water and—"

"Mitch, honey, you're white as a sheet," he said, gently catching her hand to stop her. "The ointment will be fine."

"Danny, dealing with the sight of blood may not be my forté but I can do it. Now just relax. I promise I won't pass out."

Twenty minutes later she placed a clean plaid flannel shirt over his freshly bandaged shoulder and heaved a huge sigh of relief.

"Now to bed with you," she said, and started to help him up.

"Ouch!" he muttered as they straightened up together, his right arm about her shoulders.

"Real heroes don't say 'ouch.' " She tried to lighten the mood as they headed for the bedroom. "They bite on a stick or something and don't make a sound."

"Really?" he said, pausing beside the bed to look down at her skeptically. "I've already told you I'm no hero. And, by the way, now that you've brought up the subject, just how many heroes in pain have you been companion to, missy?"

"Not many," she admitted, delighted to see the familiar twinkle back in his eyes. "But I've seen lots of old western movies."

"Well, I'm not John Wayne and there's no Apache arrow in my back," he grunted, easing himself onto the bed. "I'm just a wimpy camp patrol guy who was dumb enough to get hit with a widowmaker."

"Widowmaker?" Mitch was unfamiliar with the term.

"A tree that's ready to fall—one to be avoided, if you have a brain," he said.

Then, with a sigh of relief he stretched out on his belly on the mattress. Mitch removed the shirt she had draped around him and pulled the duvet up to his bandaged shoulders.

"Sleep," she said softly, and bent to kiss him lightly on the cheek he'd turned upward from the pillow. "Those painkillers should kick in any minute."

"Oh, right," he muttered, fisting his pillow. "Kiss me now when I'm too sore and drugged to do anything about it. You just wait till I sleep this off and see what happens."

"I'll be waiting," she purred tauntingly. "Especially to hear all about those ghosts from your past and how we're going to get rid of them."

Chapter Ten

"Constable Bradley Stuart here. Is that you, D. J.? Over."

"Brad?" In her relief, Mitch almost shouted into the mic. At that moment a chorus of angels couldn't have been any more welcome than the sound of the mountie's voice crackling over the CB radio. It had taken every ounce of her ingenuity, logic, and common sense to interpret the instructions Dan had left written on a note-pad beside the two-way contraption, and now finally, success!

"Mitch? Miss Wallace? Is something wrong? Where's D. J . . . Dan? Over."

"He's been injured," she answered, getting into the rhythm of flicking from talk to listen.

"A tree fell on him. He's sleeping now but he needs a doctor. Can you come for him? Over."

"Of course. How badly is he hurt? Should I bring a sled, or do you think he can ride a snowmobile with me? Over."

"A sled," Mitch breathed gratefully. "Most definitely, bring a sled."

Dan continued to sleep soundly and, after checking him every few minutes as she waited for Constable Stuart's arrival, she decided she must find something to quell her restlessness. The manuscript in the desk drawer fairly seemed to beckon and, after arguing with herself about her right to do so, she lost, took out the handwritten pages, and settled comfortably in the rocking chair in front of the fire. Shortly she was enthralled by the gift of a master storyteller.

Twenty minutes later Dan moaned, breaking the spell.

"Can I do anything for you?" she asked softly, sitting down on the edge of the bed and taking his hand, now fully aware of the strength and depth of his talent and completely in awe of it.

"You're doing it." He forced a wan smile and her heart fluttered at the caring in his eyes.

"Dan . . ." She wanted to confess that she'd

discovered his secret, that she was over-
whelmed by his genius, but he cut her short.

"Call me Danny," he said. "I like that. And
I'll call you Michelle. It's soft and beautiful . . . like you really are. Mitch was that
tough Toronto reporter. The name doesn't fit
anymore."

"All right . . . Danny." She drew a deep
breath, then blurted, "Danny, you're D. J.
Carson, aren't you?"

"I was trying to tell you . . . slowly," he said.
"I couldn't bring myself to say it straight out
so I started dropping clues . . . like my friendship with Brad. Then I purposely left the desk
drawer unlocked. I knew with your curiosity
you couldn't resist a peek."

"But why?" she asked, amazed. "Surely being an internationally acclaimed writer is nothing to be ashamed of."

"No, it's not," he said, watching her carefully "But after you'd told me about this Ken
Clark and how he'd recently pulled the rug out
from under you, I was afraid you'd see me in
the same light even if I did devise this subterfuge long before I met you. And then you confessed you're a member of the paparazzi, a
group I despise and, after the incident with

Mindy, had vowed never to trust or have any contact with again."

He adjusted himself on his pillows and grimaced as he continued, "I actually was able to become a colossal pain to them and enjoyed it. You see, after my books hit big-time success, I refused any and all interviews and photo sessions and thwarted them at every turn. And now I've fallen in love with one of them! Go figure."

"Love?" Her voice quavered at his words.

"Michelle, my angel." His strong warm hand enveloped her small, cold, shaky one and held it in a firm, reassuring grip. His voice ached with caring. "I love you."

She looked up at him and saw the truth of his words in his eyes.

"Danny . . ." With her free hand she reached out and gently touched his cheek.

"Say it," he muttered. "I know you can now. And mean it."

"I love you."

He smiled and closed his eyes. "Good. That's settled. Now I'm really sleepy. It must be those painkillers you fed me. But stay with me, will you?"

"Of course." Smiling tenderly, Mitch pushed tangled black hair back from his forehead, then remembered. "But, Danny, according to Ken, D. J. Carson has long blond hair and a mustache."

"Dye," he mumbled as he drifted off to sleep. "A little bottle of hair dye, a good, sensible haircut, and a shave. Not the world's greatest disguise, but apparently effective."

His breathing became deep and regular. Convinced he was resting comfortably, Mitch rose and went into the kitchen. There she stretched cramped muscles, then breathed a long, contented sigh and hugged herself happily.

"I love Danny and he loves me," she told Sadie, who had been dozing by the stove.

The little dog whined and cocked her head questioningly.

"Oh, all right." She chuckled. "He loves us. That's the deal, isn't it? Love me, love my dog. And, listen, Sadie, the storm seems to be dying down."

She went to a window and was relieved to see that the wind was abating, the sky brightening.

"Look, babe," she said. "It's over. You and Danny and I can leave whenever we want to. But," she said thoughtfully, stroking Sadie's head as the little dog braced her front paws on

the windowsill to look out beside her mistress.
"I'm not sure I want to. We're happy here,
aren't we? Like Mom and Dad were." She
chuckled when Sadie barked what sounded like
a definite affirmative.

"Brad Stuart should be here in less than an
hour now," she continued aloud to the dog.
"But I wonder if Dan made all the adjustments
necessary out at the shed to keep us function-
ing utility-wise until then. I think I'll take a
look. I managed to get that CB radio working;
maybe the city mouse can also handle a generator."

She glanced into the bedroom, saw Dan
sleeping peacefully, and decided it was a good
time to check it out. She put on her boots and
jacket and opened the door.

"Come on, Sadie," she invited. "You've
snoozed long enough. A little fresh air will do
you good."

Sadie rose from her place by the windowsill,
stretched, and jumped to the floor.

Mitch walked out onto the doorstep and
paused to survey her surroundings. It was the
first opportunity she had had to view the area.
First darkness, then snow and sleet had blan-
keted the cabin windows since her arrival.

Dan's small, weathered cabin was in a hollow at a bend of what appeared to be a wide brook. Frozen, it was a winding trail of pristine white that came from deep in the hills that bordered the little valley and led out to the river. Such a wide brook was probably fairly deep, she thought absently as she started down the steps, probably deep enough to float a canoe a good distance—

The significance of the fact galvanized her in her tracks.

"Sadie, we're in Hart's Hollow!" She gasped. "No wonder Dan knows so much about the hermit. He and Harvey are probably next door neighbors, probably co-conspirators! Dan lies for Harvey and Harvey covers up for Dan. How convenient!"

Outrage accelerating her heart rate, she barely felt the icy wind as she plodded around to the back of the cabin where an equally weathered shed snuggled under a canopy of lacy, ice-encrusted cedars. With an effort that took most of her strength, she shoved open the plank door and stepped into its dim, vaguely warm interior.

Inside she found a confusing array of fuel tanks and a piece of humming equipment she assumed was the generator. It gave off a faint aura of warmth. Extra firewood was piled in one corner, a mud-spattered motorcycle stored in another. Sadie wandered about sniffing interestedly and suddenly as she moved closer to the firewood, Mitch discovered her nose wrinkling, too.

A smell, strangely familiar and thoroughly unpleasant, wafted out from behind it. She paused, trying to place it, then suddenly, with a gasp, remembered.

Surely Harvey wasn't living out here, she thought, and immediately felt her hair prickling along the back of her neck.

"Harvey?" she called out tentatively. "Harvey, where are you?"

Sadie, who had been nosing around behind the woodpile, suddenly barked sharply.

"Sadie? What is it? Have you found him?" Cautiously she moved around the stored fuel and breathed an immense sigh of relief when she saw the pile of dirty Harvey clothes laying there.

A puzzled frown knit her brows. What were they doing there? The hermit certainly couldn't have left in his underwear, not in this weather. Yet there lay his filthy shirt and overalls and . . . she moved the pile gingerly with the toe of her boot . . . his hair and beard!

"No!" she breathed as understanding slowly came to her. "No, he couldn't . . . he wouldn't deceive me like that . . . not if he loved me!"

Chapter Eleven

"And so after Constable Stuart took Dan to the doctor, he returned to the cabin and brought you and Sadie here," Geraldine concluded a few hours later as she stirred eggs and milk into her sugar cookie batter. "After, of course, you'd made it clear to this Danny that you never wanted to see him again."

Sitting at the kitchen table in her friend's living quarters at the back of the store, Mitch took another sip of tea and nodded. "I had no choice, did I? He lied, he deceived me, he—"

"Seems to me you lied to him more than a little yourself about your reason for coming down here," Geraldine said mildly, blending the mixture carefully.

170

"I didn't concoct that lie to deceive him," Mitch shot back. "I just told you, I had to make up a reason for leaving Toronto to protect my family. So stop trying to tar me with the same brush, Geraldine. I wasn't anywhere near as deceitful as he was."

"Is that a fact?" Geraldine molded the dough into a ball and plopped it out onto a floury board. "I would have thought hiding the fact that a person is a fugitive from the law is a little more serious than pretending to be a harmless hermit who's only looking for peace and solitude. And just remember, Dan or D. J. or whatever he calls himself invented those alias before he met you, too. He never intended them to be used against someone he cared for, someone he loved. And didn't you just tell me he saved you and Sadie not once but twice? What does that say about the man's character?"

"I could go back to Toronto tomorrow," Mitch said, swirling the last drop of tea about in her cup and pretending not to hear her friend's logical arguments. "Brad told me he had a call from Capt. Matheson of the Toronto Police this morning and he told him the Toronto Police had finally gotten enough evidence on Councilor Giverson to arrest him.

Largely, I understand, through the efforts of my former colleague Ken Clark."

"So go back to Toronto." The elderly woman gave the dough a flattening slap. "Go back to your old flame. Let him get you into more messes that will hurt both you and your parents."

"What are you saying, Geraldine? That I should go back to Dan, forgive him, and live happily ever after with his lies?"

"That's got to be your decision." Geraldine picked up her rolling pin and began to make a smooth sheet of the mound. "I only know I'd hate to see you miss out on all the wonderful kind of years I had with my Stanley simply because pride and misunderstanding got in the way. Michelle, honey, I'm not your mother but I do know what she'd say if she were here."

"Which is?" Mitch lowered her eyes to her cup.

"Michelle, thirty years ago your father and mother saw each other for the very first time in this old store." Geraldine took the young woman's soft hands in her gnarled, floury ones. "Stan and I were behind the counter that day and we both saw something special flash between them right off. And you have that same look when you talk about this Danny fella. I figured you two would hit it off. That's why I got him to deliver those molasses cookies to you. I didn't know you'd already met the night before."

"So you played cupid and now you're saying if Mom were here, she'd tell me to go back to Dan, to love him like she loves Dad?" Gently Mitch extricated her hands from the elderly woman's and arose. She walked over to a window near the old-fashioned wood stove in the corner and looked out over the faded café curtains. The clouds were breaking up to let blue sky shine through.

"That's exactly right." Geraldine picked up a heart-shaped cookie cutter and inserted it carefully into the dough.

"But, Geraldine, Mom and Dad met in a different time . . . where love and commitment went hand in hand, when love was more than a physical thing, a passing moment, like it is now." Mitch ran an agitated hand through her short hair and turned back to her friend.

"And what do you think this Dan's been offering you, giving you?" The old lady was indignant as she reached for a cookie sheet. "He's always been there when you needed him. He's saved you and Sadie twice from almost certain death. And he's asked for nothing in return except your heartfelt love. If he's not a knight in shining armor on a white horse, it's only because he was born too late for the era!

"But to top if off, you run out on him when he's hurt and needs you!" Geraldine's indignation was turning to exasperation as she walloped the tin down on the table. "Right now you should be at the doctor's with him. Well, maybe just this once I was wrong. Maybe you don't deserve a fine man like Dan Jeffrey!"

"Don't deserve! What are you talking about? Didn't I care for him after that tree fell on him? Didn't I master that CB radio sufficiently to call Constable Stuart to come and take him to a doctor? Didn't Sadie and I wait alone at that isolated cabin for hours for Brad to come back for us and tell us Dan would be okay? Didn't I tell him I love him?"

"Okay, have it your way." Geraldine returned to cutting out valentine cookies and placing them on the baking sheet. "It's your life."

For a few moments there was silence punctuated only by the ticking of the antique cuckoo clock above the stove. Then Mitch turned from the window, a smile slowly spreading out like a ripple from her lips until it filled her entire face.

"You canny old sweetheart," she said softly. "You argue like a million-dollar defense attorney and make sense like a logician. Are you sure you're not a graduate of Queen's or Harvard? Maybe Oxford or Cambridge?"

"Try the eighth grade and the school of common sense." Geraldine was smiling too as she headed for the oven with a tray of cookies. "And as such, my next words of wisdom will be that you get on the phone immediately. Call Brad Stuart and ask him to take you back to that man. Right away."

"That won't be necessary."

The sound of Dan's voice made them both turn toward the curtained doorway that divided store and apartment.

"Dan." Mitch gripped the counter for support and felt her heart stick in mid-beat as she saw him framed in the entrance, his left arm in a cast and sling. "Your arm . . ."

"One small broken bone, nothing serious." he said, brushing aside her concern with a wave of his free hand. "I came upon a far more serious matter, a quest in fact. Like one of those knights Geraldine was just talking about."

"Quest?" Mitch had managed to get her

heart going again but felt as if she were resting on the quick of her soul as she stared at him.

"Yes," he said, and broke into the crooked grin Mitch couldn't resist. He pulled a gray woolen sock from behind his back and dangled it in front of her.

"I seek the lady whose dainty foot does not well fit this delicate garment," he said. "She fled before I could assure her of my undying love and capture her heart forever through blatant acts of life-threatening insanity . . . such as explaining my subterfuge."

"Dan . . ." Mitch was halfway between laughter and tears but when she made a move toward him, he halted her with an upraised hand, determined to carry out his charade to the end.

"Uh-uh, beauteous maiden. First I must be satisfied that you are indeed my one true love. Sit."

He indicated the kitchen chair she had left pulled out from the table, and she did as he wished.

Carefully he knelt, removed her moccasin, and, awkwardly using his right hand and the fingertips of his left that protruded from the bandages, slid the big sock gently over her foot.

"Ah-ha!" he exclaimed triumphantly. "A perfect misfit. You are indeed the maid of my dreams. Come live in my log cabin with me and be mine forever."

"Oh, Danny!" Mitch was laughing and crying all at once. And when he arose and drew her to her feet and against his chest a moment later, neither of them noticed Geraldine quietly slip out to the store, a sly smile of satisfaction on her lips.

Chapter Twelve

"When would you like to start interviewing me for that book you're so determined to write about my Harvey persona?" Dan asked suddenly.

"What!? You mean you're going to allow me?" Mitch looked up at him, utterly amazed.

They were seated on the threadbare love seat in Geraldine's apartment waiting for her to finish serving a customer before they left to go back upriver, Dan's right arm draped about her shoulders.

"Saving your father's business and your professional reputation is more important than my desire to hide from the media." He shrugged with an indifference Michelle knew he was far from feeling.

"Danny, you'd do that? For me?" She stroked his cheek gently with her hand.

"Should make a pretty good yarn." He grinned ruefully. "Three separate identities, how I achieved them, and went on to win the woman I love."

"No." Michelle arose and went to look out the window into a clear, sunny late afternoon. Snow crystals winked up at her from Geraldine's backyard and she felt an urge to wink back.

"I can't be hearing correctly. You don't want my story . . . after all you put yourself through to try to get it?" Dan's eyes widened. "Well, I definitely love you, woman, but I definitely don't understand you."

"Actually I can get by without it now," she said, turning back to him with a teasing little shrug of her shoulders. "Thanks to Ken Clark, Councilor Giverson is no longer a threat. I can go back to Toronto now, book or no book, no problem."

"Really?" She saw the stark disappointment in Dan's eyes and couldn't continue her teasing.

"Oh, Danny, D. J. Carson, Harvey, or whatever you choose to call yourself!" She fairly flew back to her place beside him on the couch. "As if I would, as if anything in the world could take me away from you!"

"Then what about the book? I thought you were actually interested in writing . . . something more than news stories?"

"I am." She clasped her hands about her knees in delight. "But I've discovered I don't need exposés or facts painful to anyone to write the book I'm planning. I've discovered a story I can write, that I will love to write and with no discomfort to anyone. It was right under my nose all along, only I was too busy focusing on what I thought was the big picture that I couldn't see the priceless little miniature. I'm going to write the story of this place, tales from a country store, all the yarns and bits of rural wisdom and jokes and legends that first made me want to be a writer. It's a vanishing bit of Canadiana and I plan to capture it for posterity."

"Hey, that sounds great! I'm sure my agent will be interested . . . once he forgives me for running out on him. And I'm pretty sure he will when he sees what I've come up with in my seclusion. Should give even *Star Wars* a run for its money."

"Oh, Danny, that's wonderful! When can I read it?"

"Someday soon . . . whenever you're not baking cookies." He pretended seriousness but his eyes were laughing.

"Danny, I'm sorry I yelled at you," she began. "But finding out you're three different people . . . and just after I'd grown to believe I could trust you."

"But I didn't do any of it to deceive you," he said. "You just happened along after I'd set the whole thing up."

"Geraldine made me understand that," she said softly, smiling a little as she recalled her elderly friend's words of wisdom.

"Well, bless her heart!" Dan broke into that lopsided grin Mitch found irresistible. "I will thank her profusely before we leave."

"But setting a triple identity . . . that must have taken very detailed planning," Mitch said, leaning comfortably back against him.

"Initially." He grinned, enfolding her as best he could against him. "Once I got started, though, it rolled right along. When I first made the decision to get away from the obligations of that book tour my agent and publisher had set up without my consent, I decided I'd come here to visit Brad, like I've done in the past, to get away. Only this time it somehow had to be a secret. So I decided to rent an isolated cabin Brad and I had seen while we were on a fishing trip upriver last summer and assume the identify of a burned-out recluse.

"I drove my car to Pearson Field in October and bought a ticket to Mexico. Then, instead of taking that flight I left my vehicle in the airport parking lot, picked up a U-Haul a friend had rented for me in his name, loaded a motorcycle, a snowmobile, and anything else I thought I might need including modern kitchen and bathroom fittings aboard, and headed for New Brunswick.

"Once in the province I assumed my hermit disguise. I drove to the cabin and unloaded everything but the motor bike. Then I returned the truck to one of its company depots and went back to my hideout on the bike."

"Pretty clever, but where did Dan Jeffrey the unemployed plumber-slash-camp patroller come in?" she asked.

"I soon discovered that my hermit ruse made it difficult for me to visit Brad. Not only did I enjoy those trips since they provided me with a bit of human contact, but they were necessary if I wanted to maintain a supply of clean clothes, towels, and the like. Setting up a washer and dryer here was a bit too much even for a professional plumber. So I devised the camp patrol ploy.

"At first straight-arrow Brad wasn't about to issue what he considered false ID but I finally convinced him that putting Daniel Jeffrey on a card wasn't illegal. My name actually is Daniel Jeffrey . . . Carson."

"And I *am* a plumber by trade—was working at it, in fact, right up until the day my first book hit the best-seller list. You saw my skills around your cottage and this cabin. At Brad's request, I also did some work for people in the community who were having trouble getting a plumber way down here in winter.

"Actually," he continued looking down at his work-hardened hands, "those jobs helped authenticate my disguise—gave my hands back the working-man look they used to have."

His eyes were twinkling now but Mitch had one more question.

"And Brad's refusal to lie—that's why he kept telling people simply that you weren't staying with him . . . not that you weren't in the area."

"Correct." Dan shook his head, grinning.

"Brad's in the right profession. He's the most honest man I've ever met."

"Unlike some I know," Mitch said, making a pretense at an annoyed response.

"Hey, I tried to give you a clue when I named my hermit persona Harvey. I assumed you were familiar with the Jimmy Stewart classic *Harvey*. In that movie Harvey is a huge, totally imaginary rabbit."

"Well, pardon my ignorance!" Mitch was exasperated. "I guess I'm not a very accomplished ancient movie buff! But how did you manage that awful smell?" She wrinkled her nose at the memory.

"I found a deserted bear den not far from my cabin." He chuckled. "I simply threw my Harvey gear into it and stirred. That stench did exactly what I wanted it to do: it kept you from coming too close and possibly recognizing me. If you'd ever encountered a bear's living quarters, you'd have recognized it. I just assumed you hadn't been."

"I haven't, and after smelling Harvey I don't want to—ever!" she declared emphatically.

"Well, even if you weren't familiar with the Jimmy Stewart classic, you should have been suspicious when I started calling you Michelle. You never told me your real name but you did introduce yourself to Harvey that way. I guess he scared you so much you forgot to be Mitch the Cool."

"You left a veritable potpourri of clues, it seems," she said, looking up at him, eyes narrowed. "Hmmm. That would seem to indicate a subconscious desire to be caught, definitely not a good trait in a career criminal."

"But apparently effective for a man in love trying to win his lady. Michelle?" He said it so gently, her first name sliding so tenderly from his lips, she looked up at him, startled. "How do you think a marriage between a repentant cat burglar and an inept con artist would work out?"

She paused a moment to look down at Sadie lying at their feet.

"What do you think, girl? Do you think I should marry Danny, a.k.a. D. J. Carson, a.k.a. Harvey the Hermit of Hart's Hollow?"

Sadie jumped to her feet with an enthusiastic bark.

"There you have it, sir. A definite yes if ever I heard one!" Michelle said, and embraced him carefully, her quest for the Hermit of Hart's Hollow concluded.

Later, they drove downriver on his snowmobile into a beautiful Valentine's Day winter sunset, Mitch at the controls, Dan balancing the now-veteran rider Sadie easily between them. So what if her prince was a plumber and his mount a snowmobile, not a white horse. *Hey*, she thought, *things change, even happy endings*. She and her hero were heading into a whole new millennium, weren't they? Together and forever were what really counted, just as they always had.